When *Love* Comes Home

THE FITZPATRICK FAMILY
SAMUEL & TIFFANY

judythe morgan

Published by The Danfield Press
Contact: www.judythemorgan.com

Cover Design by Jim Peto
Copy editor: Diana Peto
Interior Formatting by Bravia Books

ISBN: 978-1-7365539-4-7
First printing

Published in the United States of America.

Dedication

To missionaries everywhere.
Thank you for answering your call.
Our prayers go with you.

Deuteronomy 31:6:
"Be strong and courageous. Do not fear or be in dread of
them, for it is the LORD your God who goes with you. He
will not leave you or forsake you."

Fitzpatrick Family of Burton, Texas

Parents

Father:
Colin (Pastor Fitz)
Senior Pastor, New Hope Community

Mother:
Patricia (Ms. Pat)

Children
Matthew, Died in Afghanistan

Caleb, Burton Police Detective
Wife: Carrie, Psychologist
Child-Benjamin

Sarah, twin of Becca, Music Teacher
Husband: Nick Stephens
Step-daugher: Rachel

Becca, twin of Sarah, School Teacher
Husband: Ethan LaMotte

Andy, School Teacher
Wife-Darcy, owner Buds and Blooms

Josh, US Army Reservist
Wife-Mara, Greenview boys Home Administrator

Samuel, Missionary on Furlough
Wife-Tiffany, owner Fischler Textiles

Faith, Lawyer
Husband-Blake Robbins

Chapter 1

Sammy shoved Faith's newest purchase, a clunky, pointy dragon crafted from farm machinery parts, into her car trunk. This was his third trip to load something he didn't want to lug around. Now he understood why her husband Blake grinned when he explained he couldn't come along today. His weekend duty defending drunks and disorderly conduct soldiers meant Sammy had escorted his sister to the local craft fair.

The morning sun beat down with blinding brightness and the hot, humid air made breathing nearly impossible. "Blake got the better end of the deal," he muttered and slammed the trunk.

Swiping perspiration from his neck with his handkerchief, he returned to the vendor area where he'd left Faith shopping. She'd wandered out of sight.

Again.

He raised his hand to his forehead to block the sun and scanned the aisles. A woman holding a quilt caught his eye. Not Faith, but a shiver of familiarity crawled up his arms and down his spine.

Tiff?

Gone was the sun-lightened, blond hair he'd run his fingers through, replaced by a dark, burnished-golden, brown color. Still, the similarity was uncanny. The woman laughed at something the vendor said. The singsong sound swam through the muggy air. How long had it been since he'd heard it? Ten years? Didn't matter. He'd recognize that voice anywhere.

Tiffany Fischer. His Tiff.

Sammy couldn't take his eyes away from her as a tender sadness washed over him, remembering the divorce papers that brought him to North Carolina.

She turned his way and dazzling blue eyes, the same as he remembered, aimed his direction. Faint lines formed at the corners as she smiled. Had worry or laughter put them there?

The quilt in her hand fell into a heap. "Samuel?"

Samuel. She'd always insisted upon calling him Samuel, never Sam or Sammy. Always Samuel. Sammy made him sound like he was a ten-year-old, she'd told him.

"Tiff? Is it you?"

She rushed forward, her arms open wide. As if time and hurt had never happened, he slid into her embrace. Her arms encircled his chest, her head burrowed against his collarbone. "Samuel."

He inhaled her scent. The herbal fragrance of her shampoo filled his nose. Silky-soft curls tickled his chin. Holding her in his arms again was like she'd never left. All his dreams that she'd return come true.

She pulled her head away and stepped back just as quickly. His arms felt empty, and like in every dream he had, he woke, and she was gone.

"I can't believe this. What are you doing here?"

Her question baffled him. Her lawyer had summoned him. She had to know why he was in town. Unsure of what was going on and cautioned by Blake not to talk about the proceedings, he opted for the simple answer. "I'm visiting Faith. She married Blake Robbins. You remember Blake. He's stationed at Ft. Bragg."

"I can't believe it. Faith Ann worshipped him. And they ended up married? Wow. It's the perfect ending."

As perfect as he and Tiffany should have been. If she hadn't—

A million questions raced through his head. Before he could figure out how to ask one without being in legal trouble, a man with greying temples walked up and kissed her on the lips then swiveled toward Sammy. His lips curled in a *she's-mine, hands-off* smile.

"Samuel, this is Brendan Murphy. Brendan, Samuel Fitzpatrick. An old classmate."

Classmates? They'd been much more. Husband and wife. He swallowed the sting and extended his hand. "Nice to meet you, Brendan."

"There you are." Faith appeared at his side. "Tiffany Fischer? Imagine seeing you here. And who is this handsome gentleman?"

Brendan took Faith's hand and kissed it lightly. "Brendan Murphy and you are?"

"Faith Robbins. Sammy's sister."

Tiff's smile widened, but the sparkle fell short of her eyes. "Friends from back home." She slipped her hand through Brendan's arm. That's when Sammy caught the flash of the sparkly diamond on her left finger.

His heart tumbled down to his toes then bounced to his throat like a rubber ball. Confusion and jealousy stroked at him, teasing and taunting. He swatted the claws away.

"Let's get a lemonade and visit," Tiffany suggested.

Brendan pushed back the sleeve of his monogrammed shirt to glance at the gold watch on his wrist. "Perhaps another time. We're set for dinner, my Luv. We need to be going." His tone rumbled with impatience.

Her face flushed. "Sammy, are you going to be here long? We can all get together."

He stiffened. What game was she playing? She'd filed for divorce. He'd see her in court on Monday.

Faith placed her hand on his arm preempting a response. "He'll be here until things are settled."

Tiff's brow furled as though Faith's answer didn't make sense. She dug into her tote and pulled out a business card. "Give me a call. We'll set up lunch or something before you go back home."

Their fingers grazed and lingered. Not long. Maybe two seconds. Longing for more contact, he brushed his thumb over her soft knuckles as she released the card. A mere whisper of a touch. The contact sent a quake through his body. A flicker of awareness flashed in her dark orbs, and she sucked in a soft breath. She jerked back her hand and pivoted to give Faith a quick hug.

"Good to see you both," she said and walked away beside Brendan.

Watching their retreat, Sammy heard his heart crack. He was too late.

Faith shook her head as they disappeared into the crowd. "That was weird."

"Very. She acted like she had no idea we'd see her in court on Monday."

"Her lawyer probably told her not to talk about the divorce same as we told you."

"But she seemed genuinely happy to see me, didn't she?" He sounded like a pathetic love-struck high schooler. He was going to need to pull himself together before Monday.

"She did." Faith put her arm through his. "What say we head home and grill those steaks I thawed? Forget about Tiffany Fischer and that summons."

Faith might be able to forget, but that was never going to happen for him.

"We could have visited with them," Tiffany complained to Brendan as they walked toward the fairground exit after seeing Samuel and Faith.

"No time. We have a meeting with another distributor before the fundraiser. I thought I mentioned it."

She didn't like that he sometimes forgot to include her in his planning. "You should have told me sooner."

"Sorry. It won't take long. If things go like I think, retailers will be screaming for your landscape creations after tonight. We'll need all the outlets we can get."

Aidan, Tiff's driver, met them at the exit gate. His eyes danced with his customary smile. Some of her tension lifted as he opened the door.

"No joy?" Whenever he sensed she was frustrated,

he used the Irish phrase, asking if she'd succeeded with her task.

"It was a lovely craft fair with lots of wonderful things to see."

"But did you find any new vendors?" Brendan asked when they'd settled in the SUV.

"A couple." She pulled two cards from her purse. "Both had lovely items. They're single moms eking out a living selling at craft shows and online. Having us represent their stuff will help them have some financial freedom."

She hadn't forgotten her days of standing in booths at farmer's markets and craft shows harking her artwork. Helping others was the major reason she'd set up Fischer Textiles.

"You need more workers, not more crafty items. Everyone is going to want your textile landscapes." Brendan shrugged. "And producing more of what's profitable is what we want."

She squeezed his hand. "I think we can do both."

Chapter 2

The sun was sinking behind the rooftops and taking the heat of the day with it when Sammy joined his sister and Blake on the small patio shielded from the neighbors by storage sheds on both sides. One held their storage things. The other, the neighbors'. He dropped into the chair he'd brought from inside and sipped his iced tea.

The gas grill flared to life. Blake closed the lid and frowned. "Tiffany was at the craft show? That's odd."

"Not really. Her business is handcrafted textiles. I imagine she was looking for ideas or vendors." Faith handed Blake an iced tea. "That didn't surprise me as much as her question about why Sammy was here. Like she didn't know about the hearing."

"Oh, come on. Her lawyer filed the petition." Blake lifted the lid of the grill. "Fire's ready."

"Maybe she expected me to sign and mail the papers back." No way was he doing that. He needed to know what happened. Why she disappeared.

Faith handed Blake the plate of steaks. "Maybe. With that hunk of bling on her finger, she definitely needs a divorce. Polygamy is illegal."

"She's engaged?" Blake asked over the sizzle of steaks.

"Yep. His name's Brendan Murphy." Simply saying his name made Sammy's gut tighten into a knot.

Faith nodded. "He's older and a bit possessive from the way he whisked her off. We should check him out."

Sammy blew out a loud sigh. "This is not the way you two should be spending the first months of married life."

"Nonsense. Your matchmaking is a big reason Blake and I got back together. You deserve the same happiness. We're going to do everything we can to make that happen."

Ever since Blake and Faith discovered the annulment Tiff's father coerced them into signing ten years ago had never been filed, Sammy convinced himself he could talk Tiffany out of a divorce. They'd get back together. His years of prayers answered. All his dreams come true.

Until he'd seen that ring.

If she was engaged, she had moved on. He should sign the papers and leave. Try to get on with his life and find someone else. Let Tiff have the life she'd chosen. Morally, ethically, it was the right thing to do.

Only he couldn't. His heart wouldn't let him because hearts could be tricky and stubborn and his would always want Tiff.

Tiffany sat at the head table beside Brendan at his annual black-tie benefit auction. She recognized buyers from exclusive boutiques, celebrities, and Brendan's circle of moneyed friends seated at tables with sparkling Fostoria crystal vases of fresh calla lilies. Bidding paddles rose as items being auctioned were walked across the stage.

Brendan's world. Hers now. Seeing Samuel earlier reminded her of what her life had been like.

And him. The years had broadened his shoulders, muscled his chest. A scruffy beard now framed his face, but those blue Irish eyes that stayed glued to her still made her heart flicker the same as ever. With a little mental shake, her gaze returned to the stage, but she wasn't seeing the artwork, she was seeing two teenagers standing in the Justice of the Peace's living room saying their vows. They'd been young and naïve. Full of dreams and plans.

Her dream of owning a textile business came true. She'd started Fischer Textile on a shoestring budget selling her handcrafted, one-of-a-kind items. Slowly she'd enlisted a handful of women who knitted and weaved, creating products in their homes. Under Brendan's tutelage, she'd grown to be a player in a very competitive market. What became of Samuel's plans? Was he married? Children? She wished she'd asked.

Brendan nudged her thigh. "Are you paying attention? Your donation is up next."

This year she'd contributed a woven fiber wall hanging of the Cliffs of Moher in Ireland. Brendan wanted to take her design idea, outsource it, and set up a line of wall hangings featuring domestic and foreign landscapes. That meant a new direction for Fischer Textiles—mass-produced designs. Although she trusted Brendan, new and different made her nervous.

On the other hand, mass production could mean more jobs for single women and new mothers like those two she met today at the craft show and that was the reason she'd started Fischer textiles.

It was all good.

"Next, we have this Fischer Textiles incredible mixed medium piece created by Tiffany Fischer, Mr. Murphy's fiancée. Come to the mic, Ms. Fischer, and tell us about this fabulous wall hanging."

A rush of white-crested rapids erupted in her tummy. Public speaking was not her thing. The quiet solitude of her weaving loom was her introverted self's happy place. Pasting a smile on her face, she pushed to her feet and went to the podium.

"This is my favorite work." She laughed. "I know I say that every year. But this one truly is. On a recent trip to visit Brendan's family in Ireland, we visited the Aran Islands. I watched eighth-generation knitters spin wool and knit the most exquisite sweaters. We saw hand-carved stone crosses with Celtic designs. Their craftsmanship is remarkable, but the Cliffs of Moher across the way were even more amazing. When we returned home, I had to recreate what I'd seen."

She removed the sheet to reveal a three-by-five-foot textile rendering of "The Cliffs." Oohs and ahhs echoed through the audience.

"Magnificent! Thank you, Ms. Fischer." The auctioneer took the microphone. "We had a pre-emptive bid of $50,000. The board rejected it. We're counting on raising more tonight. Do I hear sixty?"

Bidding paddles rose. Brendan's shot up first.

Tiffany returned to her seat. Her ears rang with the sound of bid numbers going higher and higher which proved Brendan was right. Landscape wall hangings could be profitable.

"Going once, going twice. Sold to Mr. Murphy."

"Your wedding gift, my Luv," Brendan said as she sat beside him.

Tiffany leaned forward and kissed him softly. "Thank you. I did hate to give it up."

"I know. Now you'll always have it to inspire you."

The auctioneer ended the auction and instructed the winners on collecting their items. Brendan pulled her to her feet. "Time to let everyone meet the artist and drum up sales."

Faith pointed at her stiletto heels. "Do we have to? I'd really like to go home, kick these off, and soak in the jacuzzi."

"Yes, we must." He took her hand in his and drew it to his lips. "Later we'll relax, promise."

Her toes screamed as she walked beside him. She accepted his extrovert to her introvert as part of what she loved about him, but sometimes it was harder than others.

Chapter 3

Monday afternoon Sammy slid onto the public benches in the tomblike courtroom beside Blake and Faith. He could hear his breath in the quiet. When the clerk called his case number, he rubbed his palms on his slacks and followed his sister and brother-in-law through the bar gate between the waiting seats of the gallery into the case presentation area. The squeaky hinge echoed in the hollow silence.

Blake directed Sammy to the defendant's table and approached the judge's bench along with Tiffany's lawyer, Gene Farrell. Sammy sat beside Faith. Tiffany was nowhere to be seen.

That seemed strange. "Shouldn't Tiff be here?" He whispered behind his cupped hand.

"The rules must be different in North Carolina. That's what Blake is talking to the judge about."

Whatever Blake said to the judge, Tiffany's lawyer sure didn't like it. He crossed his arms and threw up his chin. The judge stood and called Sammy's name. "Please join us in my chambers."

Faith rose with him. "Okay if I come, Your Honor?"

His grey head nodded.

Wall-to-ceiling bookshelves and diplomas lined the judge's chamber, but not a single window. Sammy cringed. How did anyone work all day without ever looking out to see the sky?

Blake introduced Faith once they were inside.

"Nice to meet you. Please be seated." The judge nodded then pointed to two chairs.

Blake and the other lawyer remained standing in front of the mahogany desk, which was the size of an ocean liner. Stacks of files and open law books filled the desktop. Sammy rubbed at the dry cuticle on his thumb waiting for what came next.

Gene Farrell began. "Your honor, this is a simple signoff—"

"I'll decide that." The judge cut him off. "You say this marriage took place ten years ago and the couple has never lived together?"

"That's correct, your honor," Tiff's lawyer answered. "A simple signature and we can be done."

Blake cleared his throat. "It's not quite that simple, Your Honor. Mr. Fitzpatrick was unaware that he and Ms. Fischer are still legally married. That makes a difference."

"There was an annulment, Your Honor," Mr. Farrell's voice rose a decibel. "But for whatever reason, no paperwork was ever recorded. The marriage was over before it began. Mr. Fitzpatrick just needs to sign and end this."

The judge's forehead scrunched until his bushy eyebrows nearly touched. Creases wrinkled his forehead in a frown aimed at Sammy. "All that true, Mr. Fitzpatrick?"

Sammy stood to answer. "Yes, Sir, but I've never stopped loving Tiffany."

"Then why agree to an annulment in the first place?"

Sammy fidgeted, shifting his weight from foot to foot. "We ran away on graduation night because Tiff had to leave for orientation at the University of North Carolina, Chapel Hill the next day. She had a full scholarship and her classes started that summer. She was, is, incredibly talented." He looked up at the judge. "Our plan was for me to join her as soon as I had enough money saved to get us someplace to live, but her dad insisted she'd lose her scholarship if the university found out she was married. He demanded we sign annulment papers. I wanted her to have the opportunity to do what she loved. I signed. We planned to re-marry once she graduated."

This time he wasn't signing anything. Engagement ring or no engagement ring.

"But you didn't go after her?"

"Not right away. I wrote, and I called. When she stopped returning my calls, I hitchhiked to Chapel Hill. She'd left the dorm with no forwarding address. I didn't know what else to do. I quit trying and tried to focus on my studies." He stared down at his feet. "I gave up too quickly."

Judge Hunt scowled at Tiff's lawyer. "Where is your client?"

"Mr. Murphy had a meeting."

"Mr. Murphy? Who's Mr. Murphy? Ms. Fischer's the one getting a divorce. Where's she?"

Mr. Farrell flinched, a tiny grimace that Sammy wouldn't have noticed if he hadn't been staring at the man. "Mr. Murphy is her fiancé. He hoped we could take care of the situation without involving her. She's very busy."

Judge Hunt inhaled deeply. "Too busy for her own divorce?"

"She's not aware of these proceedings," Farrell blurted.

Silence fell on the room like a guillotine.

A rock band drummer pounded in Sammy's chest. Blake's voice tunneled through the noise. "Your Honor, in light of this new information, I'd like to ask for a continuance until Ms. Fischer is informed of the proceedings and can be present."

"Absolutely." Judge Hunt pushed from his chair, leaned forward on the desk, and nailed Mr. Farrell with a murderous look. "This may be a family court, but you're pulling none of your fancy New York shenanigans in my court. I want Ms. Fischer here. Tomorrow. In my chambers."

Judge Hunt pushed around his desk and marched over to the bailiff. "Put them on tomorrow's docket."

The two men left the room, and the door swished closed.

Mr. Farrell threw papers into his briefcase before he stormed across the room. At the door, he turned to Sammy. "Don't get your hopes up, Mr. Fitzpatrick. Ms. Fischer is committed to Mr. Murphy and he to her."

Sammy slumped in his chair and gripped the arms to steady the spinning in his head.

"We'll talk in the car." Blake led the way out of the courthouse.

Faith slammed her car door and yanked the seatbelt across her lap. "Can you believe that? Brendan Murphy is a jerk."

Sammy finally found his voice. "That doesn't give him the right to do a dirty thing like this."

"No, it doesn't. I think he's afraid he'll lose Tiffany." Faith turned and winked at him. "Don't give up, little brother."

Chapter 4

Tiff hadn't asked for this divorce.

Sammy's seesaw world took another sudden dive and bounced hard with the realization. Did that mean there was a chance?

Hope slammed into him like a freight train. He stared out the rear car window, not seeing anything as the possibility settled in his mind.

In the front seat Faith and Blake discussed the unusual situation. "If Tiff didn't file for the divorce, then she probably doesn't know they're still married."

"That's what I'm thinking. But we can't be sure. It might be she couldn't face Sammy." Blake flashed his ID at the Ft. Bragg gate. The guard waved him through. Minutes later, he shifted into park in front of the on-post family condominium he'd managed to secure on short notice from one of the sergeants who owed him a favor.

"If Tiff doesn't know about the divorce, that's good, isn't it?" Sammy watched both their shoulders rise and fall in a shrug duet.

Faith shifted to face him. "It all boils down to her reaction when she finds out."

"Exactly," Blake said. "And we have no clue what that reaction will be."

"She's got to be upset with that Brendan guy because he didn't tell her. Maybe if I talked to her..." If there was the slimmest chance she'd come back to him, Sammy planned to pursue it.

"Right. That's the challenge." Blake opened his car door.

Faith put her hand on his forearm and tilted her head toward their quarters' front door. A woman stood holding a covered dish between hot pads in her hands. "We'll talk later. Army bases are small towns on steroids. You don't want to feed the gossip wind." She led the way to greet the woman.

Dimples formed in the brunette's plump cheeks when she smiled at Sammy. "You must be Faith's brother. I'm Ava. Sorry for your troubles."

Sammy muttered a thank you and trailed Blake inside. Faith followed minutes later and set the casserole on the counter. "Her yummy lasagna."

"That was a quick visit... for Ava." Blake passed silverware to Sammy.

Faith winked. "I didn't invite her in this time. She's been feeding us since we moved in," she added as an aside to Sammy.

Blake grabbed plates from the kitchen cabinet. "She's a fantastic cook. Almost as good as Ms. Pat and Rose. I'm not complaining."

"You're right. She'd kind and would anything to help someone in need." Faith sliced the lasagna. "We just don't need her hanging around all the time."

Blake handed her a plate. His fingers lingered on her hand. His thumb caressed the soft skin at her wrist in an intimate way, and the look that passed between them put a radiant glow on her face.

Guilt zinged Sammy. He was just as much an intruder as Ava. His sister and her husband should be having quiet, romantic newlywed dinners alone... not spending their time sorting through his mess.

Sammy wasn't sure what he expected to see when he walked into the courtroom the next day. The woman with her hair in a twist updo, wearing a black tailored suit from a fashion magazine his sisters poured through, sure wasn't on his radar. Day before yesterday Tiff had worn jeans and a tank top at the craft show, her blonde hair swishing softly at her shoulders. That Tiff he remembered. This Tiffany Fischer—all model-like sophisticated and poised, was out of his league. He didn't recognize her. Didn't know her.

"Samuel." She hardly looked at him as she took her place at the plaintiff table. Her voice sounded formal like he was a stranger she was meeting for the first time, not the man she'd married.

Stunned and hurt, his voice came out like he had a mouthful of socks. "Tiff."

Judge Hunt stood. "To my chambers, gentlemen."

Blake and Farrell motioned the others to follow.

Once inside the judge's chambers, he directed them to opposite sides of a wide, rectangular table. Tiff, Brendan, and her lawyer on one side. Sammy, Blake, and

Faith on the other. Like football players lined up awaiting the referee's whistle.

Mr. Farrell cleared his throat. "As you can see by the affidavit, Your Honor. Ms. Fischer—"

Judge Hunt raised his hand, stopping him. "I've read the affidavit. I want to hear from Ms. Fischer. Why are you seeking a divorce after ten years?"

"I didn't know I even needed one until last night. Brendan and his lawyer told me what they discovered." She kept her eyes down, her words soft, hoarse.

Judge Hunt's pursed his lips but said nothing as she continued.

"I had no idea Samuel and I... were... we are... still married. It was a surprise." She twisted her engagement ring. Her forehead wrinkled.

"Does finding out make a difference?"

Her gaze met Sammy's. "I don't know...yes...of course, I'd never..."

Brendan clasped his hand over hers. "Your Honor, what the lass is trying to say is she'd have sought a divorce before she accepted my proposal. She's not that kind of woman."

"No one is suggesting she is. What I'm trying to figure out here is if the fact you kept the marriage from her is a problem?"

Mr. Farrell's shoulders rose as he inhaled. "Sir, I'm not sure that has any bearing here. The whole purpose of this hearing is to get a signature from Mr. Fitzpatrick on the divorce decree."

"Let me explain." Judge Hunt's tone was a barely concealed threat. "Her feelings are important. Very important. I don't grant any divorce lightly. Bit of peculiarity I have. You, not being from around here, wouldn't know that."

Farrell shook his head, then muffled a snort and leaned back in his chair.

"I thought not. This woman has not had proper time to assimilate what she's just learned. Your client," Judge Hunt's gaze swept toward Sammy, "and this gentleman have the right to process this whole mess of still being married before they leap into a divorce. Wouldn't you say?"

Brendan's shoulder went up, his chest puffed out. "Bullocks. Doesn't matter. They haven't laid eyes on each other in ten years. She's loving me now."

Sammy recognized his Irish temper coming through. Whenever his dad got upset or frustrated, he slid into Irish phrasing too.

The judge's gavel boomed. "You were gonna deny them the opportunity to be sure they even want a divorce by tricking her?"

Brendan's cheeks flushed. "I'll not be tricking her. I'll be protecting her."

"Well, Mr. Murphy, you're gonna need to explain exactly what you are protecting her from. She deserves to know. I'm delaying my decision for six weeks to give all y'all time to get this figured out." The sleeve of Judge Hunt's black robe swept the table as he pointed to Tiffany, then Sammy. "And you two need to do some talking too."

He pushed from the table and swept out the door like a great wizard with his robe sleeves flapping behind him.

"He can't do that," Brendan protested.

Blake shrugged. "He just did. Judge Hunt is known

for his unorthodox ways. You and your lawyer should have researched who you were dealing with before you started. Showing up without Ms. Fischer—I mean, Mrs. Fitzpatrick— and keeping her in the dark about what was going on, you were asking for trouble. You're lucky he didn't deny your petition altogether."

"Do something, Farrell." Brendan tugged Tiff from her chair. "Let's go."

Sammy sprang to his feet, blocking their path. "Perhaps we could grab that lemonade?"

Tiff nodded. "You have my card, Samuel, call me."

Brendan puffed like a gorilla. In a small chilling voice, he locked gazes with Sammy. "And you and I will be talking too. To you, I have a lot to say."

Smiling, Faith pointed a finger at Blake when the door closed behind them. "You knew Judge Hunt would do this."

Blake smiled. "Not my first divorce case before Hunt."

"Why didn't you say anything?" Sammy asked.

"No point in raising your hopes. Ten years is a long time. Brendan may be right, and she loves him now." Blake stuffed papers in his briefcase.

Faith's fist flew to her hips. "Are you daff? Don't listen to him, Sammy. She's not going to stay with that man."

Blake snapped his briefcase closed. "That's a real possibility. You never get over your first love. I speak from experience. I didn't and I got lucky." He winked at his bride and turned to Sammy. "You were Tiff's first love. Hearts don't forget our first loves. You two need to talk and quickly."

That was Sammy's plan. He wouldn't give up easily again. He wouldn't lose her this time.

Chapter 5

"When were you going to tell me?" Tiffany whirled to face Brendan as soon as they entered his house. She'd held her tongue in front of Aidan. As her driver, he was privy to enough of her life, but this? This was too much. How could Brendan keep this from her? Why?

He shrugged. "Truthfully, I was hoping the judge would grant the divorce. We'd be married. You'd never have to know."

Her nails dug into her palms. "How dare you."

"How dare I?" He moved to tower over her. "You never even mentioned your marriage."

She cocked her head, stared at him for a long, discomforting breath. "I didn't think it was necessary. We were in high school. Dad had the marriage annulled."

The twinge of hurt that Samuel had signed the papers and never followed through on their plans stabbed her heart again. He never came for her like he promised. She inhaled a deep breath. Better to shelve what happened in the past and forget about it altogether. Like it never happened. Not exactly what her therapist said, but it had gotten her through the tough days.

"Well, Farrell couldn't find any record of an annulment when he worked up our prenup."

"But Dad gloated. Said it proved he didn't love me."

She'd wandered lost, unfocused for over a year before she snapped out of her depression. It didn't make sense he'd never filed the paperwork. "I can't understand why he didn't file."

"Doesn't matter. What's done's done. We must concentrate on getting Fitzpatrick's signature." He inched closer, draped his arms over her shoulders, and rested his forehead against hers. "Once he signs, we can be married and move on with our lives."

Still reeling from his underhandedness, Tiffany flipped his arms off and pulled away. Insisting she play *hostess with the mostess* was one thing. Keeping something like this from her was a whole different level.

She glared at him. "I think you better go."

"But we're meeting..." Shock registered in his plea.

"You handle it. Just go."

"Tiffany, I only—"

"Brendan don't press your luck. What you did was despicable and you know it. Go."

"I'll not be giving up. Fitzpatrick will sign the petition. We'll be marrying."

The door clicked closed.

Tiffany sank onto the leather sectional and dropped her head into her hands, pressing two fingers up and down her forehead. A gazillion questions tornadoed through her brain. Questions she thought she'd put to rest long ago. Had Samuel known all along? Was he married? Was that why he hadn't bothered to find her?

Too many unanswered questions.

She popped up, called Aidan's cell, and told him to tell Brendan to get a taxi. She wanted him to drive her to the farm.

Unlike this house that Brendan bought for her, everything at the farm was hers. All hers. Here Brendan selected the location and the furnishings, everything. His presence and scent were wherever she looked, even when he wasn't. She'd bought the farm she called her studio with the insurance settlement. There she could think and create and forget the world.

She'd stumbled upon the place on one of Aidan's countryside rides to cheer her up after the accident. The hand-painted FOR SALE sign had dangled from a tilting picket. The place was rundown for sure but inviting with the wraparound porch and rockers desperately in need of paint. Aidan drove her past every day for a month before he convinced her she should go inside and talk to the owners.

The moment Aidan had pushed her wheelchair over the threshold, she'd fallen in love with the quaint little farmhouse and worked out a deal. Between physical therapy and rehab, it had taken over a year to update the place before she could move in. Aidan lived in an apartment beside the barn overseeing the remodel for her.

Once she'd gotten back on her feet, he'd stayed on adding the duties of goat herder and gardener to physical therapist and chauffeur. "Like being home in County Clare," he'd said. After trips to Ireland with Brendan she'd understood why.

They made the ride to the farm in silence. Aidan didn't ask questions. After all these years, he knew when to offer conversation and when to just drive. He unloaded her case and disappeared.

Tiffany walked into the room that was as familiar to her as the sight of her face in the mirror every morning. She went straight to her loom, picked up the bobbin, and sat, staring out the windows at the goats. The usual magic eluded her. Her inspiration sucked away.

She dropped the bobbin on the loom, walked to the large picture window, and squeezed her eyes shut. "Hurry up and call, Samuel."

After finishing the neighbor Ava's leftover lasagna for lunch the next day, Blake went to his office.

Sammy lingered at the table replaying the courtroom scene and the way Brendan manipulated Tiffany. He pulled the card she'd given him that day at the craft fair from his pocket.

"You okay?" Faith asked.

He shrugged. "Confused."

"Come on. It's too nice to be inside. Let's sit out here and talk." Faith slid the patio door open and pointed to the Adirondack chairs on the little patio.

"Ya-hoo, goodies coming in." Ava came around the storage unit separating her condominium from Blake and Faith's. She handed Faith the tray of cookies she carried and unfolded the webbed lawn chair tucked under her arm.

Faith set the cookie plate on the crate serving as a

patio table. "Woman, you are spoiling us."

"That's my job. What are you two up to this afternoon?"

"I'm going online to find a place to live for the next six weeks." Sammy bit into a cookie. "Hmm. Delicious."

"You don't have to do that. You're welcome to stay with us." Faith spoke around the cookie in her mouth.

Sammy shook his head. "Too long for newlyweds to have company. I'll find something."

"Why six weeks? What happened?" Ava's aluminum chair creaked as she leaned forward for a cookie.

"The judge deferred his decision on the divorce." Faith grinned at Sammy. She'd warned him her neighbor would be direct. She'd pulled Faith and Blake's life story out of his sister in record time and Faith held things close.

"You musta had Judge Hunt. You poor thing."

Sammy wasn't sure the delay was a terrible thing. He wanted to talk with Tiff and figure out what had happened all those years ago. The judge's decree made it possible.

"They didn't know they were still married," Faith clarified for Ava.

"Her father made us sign an annulment ten years ago. Only he never filed it."

"Sounds like a mess. I'd like to help you out with a place to stay."

"What do you mean?"

"Thad and I own a duplex in town. I live there when he's deployed. Chaplain Mike and his group use the other half for families in need. Both sides are empty right now. You could use our half."

"I didn't know Mike's group had a sanctuary place," Faith said. "That's wonderful."

"Better for us. Renters sometimes trash a place. Mike's group always does clean-up. It's yours rent-free if you want, Sammy. Thad's gonna be stateside for now."

"That's very generous of you," Faith said.

"Not really. You're the generous one. Volunteering lawyer services for Mike's group, that's generosity. They'd never afford legal advice otherwise."

Faith shrugged. "Knowing your legal options makes a tough situation better. I'm happy to help with that."

"You think you'd want to have a look, Sammy?" Ava asked. "I can't guarantee how long the chaplain's side will be empty. You're welcome to our side though."

"I'd love to. I'll get my car keys."

Hours later, Sammy stuffed his clothes into the bedroom chest. Even though he'd been single for twenty-eight years and managed to survive, Ava had taken him through the two-bedroom place like it was a ten-room mansion pointing out all the things she thought he'd need to know to be on his own. It was like having his mom with him.

Faith finally convinced Ava he'd be fine and they left.

Sammy poured a glass of iced tea he'd made using the coffee maker Ava had shown him how to use, as if he'd never seen one before. He didn't have the heart to tell her all he needed was coffee for breakfast. He only drank iced tea after that.

Drink in hand, he settled on the leather couch to figure out what he was going to do next.

Chapter 6

Sammy set his mug on the coffee table and pulled Tiff's card from his wallet. Slowly he entered her information into his contacts. His finger hovered over her name when he finished while his heart battled with his brain.

Ten long years and zero contact.

Why should he barge into her world again? *Sign the papers and move on.* He set the phone down and sipped his iced tea.

But, his heart argued, how can she love such a controlling man? He'd seen the way Brendan had ushered her away when they'd met at the fair, and then again in the judge's chamber. His Tiffany would never have allowed that kind of manipulation. What had changed her?

He paced, berating himself for not trying harder to find her all those years ago. Even if she rejected him, he needed answers.

He picked up his phone, closed his eyes, and pressed her mobile number before he chickened out.

Tiff answered on the first ring. Like she'd been watching her phone. Waiting for his call. That sent a flash flood rise to his heart rate and jitters to his stomach.

"Tiff, it's Sammy." He grimaced. Shouldn't have said Sammy. She didn't like his nickname. Always said it made him sound like he was a six-year-old.

"Hi, Samuel. I'm glad you called." Her voice sounded sincere. More relief rushed through him in waves. He'd feared she wouldn't answer.

"I was wondering when we could get together to talk." The words gushed out without the polish he'd practiced. He rubbed his hand down his pants leg, holding his breath.

"How about breakfast tomorrow? Where are you staying? We can meet."

A hint of the Texas twang he remembered floated in her vowels. The cadence sounded like music to his soul. The sophisticated businesswoman he'd seen in court had not completely swallowed the sweet, hometown girl he'd married. His hopes advanced an octave.

Maybe she hadn't forgotten their past. Maybe she still loved him. Maybe…

"I'm in a duplex in town that belongs to Faith and Blake's neighbor. I'm not familiar with the area yet."

"That's okay. You have a car?"

"I do. I drove from Burton."

"Great. There's a popular diner near my farm. It's not too far outside the city limits. Let me give you the address."

He scrambled for paper and pencil, settling for a grocery ad from the stack of junk mail he'd gathered from Ava and Thad's mailbox. "Go."

She shared the address and some landmarks to watch for along the route.

"Got it. Is eight too early?"

"Eight's good. See you tomorrow."

He felt something stir inside his chest. Fragile, and whisper-thin, but glowing steadily.

Hope.

Between the firm mattress on the strange bed and his apprehension about meeting Tiff, he didn't sleep much. Giving up at first light, he left early. Good thing too. He drove past Backwoods Grill and had to backtrack. The gravel parking lot behind the structure was full for a weekday morning.

He found a space in the last row and heard gurgling water when he stepped out of his car. Because he was early, he went to explore.

A shallow creek rushed over rocks reminding him of the spring-fed pond back home. He let the gentle sound soothe him for several minutes before walking back to the rustic structure with the redwood deck across the back.

The clatter of dishes and chatter of customers combined with the scents of bacon and coffee filled his ears and nostrils when he entered. A sign instructed him to wait to be seated. Within a minute, a server carrying a coffee carafe greeted him.

"I believe Tiffany Fischer made reservations."

"Oh, yes. Tiffany's one of our regulars. Follow me." The short, curvy girl with chipmunk cheeks smiled and spoke to customers by name as she zigzagged her way to a deck door and seated him at a table off to the side.

Sammy smiled at the location. Tiff still preferred being away from crowds. He sat where he could watch the driveway entrance and waited. He had no inkling about how this morning would go.

Shortly, a black Mercedes SUV pulled up. A chauffeur opened the back door and Tiff appeared. As if sensing his presence, she looked up to the deck and waved. A good sign.

With his arms hanging awkwardly at his side, he rose when she approached the table. He wasn't sure whether to hug her or shake her hand.

She slid her briefcase-sized purse onto the empty chair and sat across from him. "Thank you for coming," she said after the server filled her mug. "Backwoods Grill has the best coffee in all of North Carolina."

Sammy lifted his cup in an affirmative salute. "It's wonderful. Dark and rich like in Guatemala."

Over the rim of his cup, he analyzed the woman, looking for his high school sweetheart. The one he'd vowed to love until death do us part and still did. Sunlight highlighted a faint, narrow, pink scar line along her neck when she brushed her hair over her shoulder. From what, he wondered. A shadow of sadness darkened the clear, sparkling blues that plagued his dreams.

The faint babbling of the creek offered a soft background for the tweeting birds and nattering squirrels and thankfully filled the awkward silence that rose between them.

"Tiff."

"Samuel." They spoke at once.

"You first," she said.

Mountains of memories rose in his head. Times

spent sharing their deepest wants and desires. Times she'd been his comfort and hope. It had taken years for him to accept she was gone forever. He never expected to ever see her again. Then whammy! He learned they are still married. He needed to understand how that had happened. He lifted his chin to project more confidence than he felt. "I was going to ask—"

"The usual today, Miss Tiffany?" The same young server smiled at them both.

"With a side of grits for Samuel, too, please." Nodding, a nostalgic smile curved her lips.

She hadn't liked grits when they'd eaten at Feelin' Good Café in Burton. He would eat a bowl every chance he got. It had been a long-running joke between them and she'd remembered. Some of the tension squeezing his chest eased. "You're having grits too?"

"I am." A smile brightened her face.

"I'm surprised. I didn't think you'd ever change your mind. White mush, you used to say."

"We've both changed. A lot." In her expressive eyes, he could see the internal war she waged. Discuss their changes more, or respect his privacy? The same dilemma he felt.

The food's arrival delayed any discussion. He dabbed a lump of butter on his grits then scooped a spoonful into his mouth. His eyes closed as he relished the taste of the best grits he'd ever eaten. "Delicious."

"I know. It's why I'm here about every day."

"You said you live nearby."

"Yes, not far. I'll show you after we eat. You can see where I work."

"Sure." Samuel looked around, seeing all the people who could overhear things. This was not a conversation they should have in public. Asking his questions in the privacy of her home would be much better.

Chapter 7

Tiffany stood after they finished a second cup of coffee. "You want to ride with me? Aidan can bring you back after we finish if you want."

"Sure. That'd be fine." Mentally, he added "Why do you use a chauffeur?" to his growing list of questions.

Aidan opened her door. "This is Samuel, Aidan."

He tipped his cap. "And pleased I am to meet you."

"Likewise." Sammy returned his nod.

Twenty minutes later, Aidan pulled the car into the driveway of a farm that looked a lot like Sammy's family home in Texas. Large oaks and fields stretched long and wide on either side of the house. The only thing missing was the church building down the road.

She slipped out the door Aidan opened. The sound of bleating filled the air.

"Call whenever you're ready to go. I'll take you back to your car." He tipped his hat to Sammy and disappeared.

Tiff escorted Sammy through the gate and motioned for him to follow her around the corner of the wraparound porch. The bleating sound got louder as the backyard came into view where a half dozen goats nibbled grass or played king of the mountain on a jungle gym-looking apparatus in a fenced area not far from the house. Chickens wandered outside the goat pen. In a small garden, corn stalks and pole beans towered over tomatoes, squash, and zucchini plants.

An Old English sheepdog the size of a Shetland pony romped across the field to join them. "This is Moo," Tiff said as the dog came to a stop at her feet and sat.

The sheepdog nosed Sammy's hand wanting a pet. "Nice to meet you, Moo." He scratched behind the dog's fluffy white ear and looked up at Tiff. "You live on a farm? I expected a city apartment above your studio like you always talked about."

"Plans and dreams have a way of changing. When Aidan and I drove by on one of my afternoon drives, I knew it was where I wanted to live and work. My parents had passed. Living in their house..." Her voice trailed off. She straightened her shoulders and continued, "I sold it, left Chapel Hill and its hard memories behind, and bought this place. The goats and vegetable garden came later."

"Your parents are gone. I didn't know. I'm sorry."

"Let's sit out here a while," she said as though she hadn't heard his condolences.

She led him up the stairs to a small table in a screened portion of the porch and motioned him to sit. "If I don't go to Backwoods, this is where I have breakfast." Moo settled at her feet.

"Nice. Moo's a strange name for a dog. Is there a story?"

"When I brought him home from the breeder, Aidan took one look at the size of her paw and said she's gonna be big as a cow. Let's call her Moo." She ruffled the dog's head. "I figured why not?"

"Mara's son Cody named the dog Josh got him Bear. I thought that was unique. Moo beats it. So, you run the farm in addition to your textile business?"

"More like a hobby. It just happened. When my therapist came out to see where I lived, she recommended I get some chickens. Then I fell in love with the little goats in the petting zoo at the local farmers' market where I sell my stuff and decided to add a few." Her gaze traveled to the pen of goats. "Fortunately, Aidan's family in Ireland raises sheep. He knows how to manage a farm while I weave and create."

"He lives here with you?" The possibility sent a jab of jealousy through him.

Tiff's eyebrows rose. "He has an apartment over by the barn. I live in the house."

"Oh." Sammy dipped his head.

"Come inside. I'll show you around."

She gave him a tour around the small farmhouse, ending in the studio room with her loom at the back of the clapboard house. He stood next to her, hands tucked in his pockets, and stared out through the picture window at the pastoral scene. Puffy, white clouds dotted the azure sky above treetops. Goats butted horns with one another and climbed the jungle gym. A carefree and happy scene.

"What a fabulous view you have while you work. It's like the world is far, far away."

And that view had helped her regain her equilibrium after the accident.

"I've tried to recreate it at my loom many times. It's impossible. But you're right, it is quite soothing." Sadness drifted through her words as the early years of coming to the farm pushed through the stonewalled recesses of her mind where she kept them locked away. She prayed that peace and contentment would fully return one day.

"Tiff, I'm sorry all this is happening. I wish—" Samuel turned to her.

She blinked away the tear trying to slip from the corner of her eye. "Wishes are a waste. At least in my experience. You accept what is and go on." His face bleached. "No. No. I didn't mean you. Or us. This…"Her hand swished between them. "We have to sort out whatever this is."

"What are you wishing for? Do I need to sign the papers and leave?"

"Honestly, I don't know. I thought everything was settled. My past done. What happened? Why didn't you come like you promised?"

He flinched. The accusation in her questions stung. "I did. But it took a while to save enough for our rent until I could find a job. When you stopped answering my letters, I hitchhiked to Chapel Hill but you'd gone. No one would give me your address. Where were *you*?"

"It's a long, complicated story. Come let's sit." Tiffany pointed toward the fireplace at the end of the long room. A rattan hammock chair hung on a stand on one side. Along the opposite wall, a love seat with her grandmother's handstitched quilt rumpled on it. She'd fallen asleep there last night. She pulled the cover off, folded it onto the stack of quilts in the basket beside the arm. "You can sit here."

"Thank you. Me and hammock chairs are not a good mix as I'm sure you remember."

She chuckled. Her dad had hung one on their porch in Burton for her. Samuel never could get in or out gracefully. "I do remember. You fell out more than once."

"Mostly because those things are designed for one person and you always climbed in with me. You never could sit still." He winked at her as he settled on the loveseat. "Nice to see you funneled all that energy into fulfilling your dream."

Their gazes clung together, a strong and tangible pull of attraction, and not just emotional, but physical too. Inhaling deeply, she settled into the rattan cocoon. Moo rested her head on her lap for a second before settling at her feet. "What about your dreams? Did they come true?"

"Mostly. After you left, I drove your folks crazy checking on you. Then they disappeared too. They moved to Chapel Hill?"

Her eyes turned downward to watch her hands smooth her skirt. "Dorm living wasn't quite what I thought it'd be. All the freedom got the better of me. My grades slipped. They moved and made me live with them." She wished it had been that simple, but that was not a story she was ready to share. "Did you make it to Guatemala?"

"I did. And it is as beautiful as all those pictures we poured over. I'm on furlough now, helping Josh and Mara at Greenvine." His words carried the same happy tone hers had when she found the farm. He'd fulfilled his dreams too.

"I found several of my vendors in Guatemala. They do such beautiful work." The hammock chair swayed as Tiff shifted. Hoping to divert him from the hard question of why she hadn't contacted him, she asked, "Josh and Mara are running the camp together? How'd that happen?"

"It's not a summer camp anymore. Mara converted it into a home for troubled boys. An alternative to foster care. Josh moved out there after a grass fire and started helping her with the boys. They ended up getting back together. But that's a story for another time. Why didn't you try to connect with me while you were in Guatemala? It's a small country."

Guilt tightened in her chest. She licked her lips. "It was only a quick trip."

"And we were together." Brendan strolled into the room.

Tiffany stiffened. "What are you doing here?" Moo repositioned herself between and Brendan.

"When you didn't come home last night, I came looking. I knew ya'd be here or at Backwoods. Him I didn't expect." He sneered at Samuel. "Did you forget our meeting with the bank?"

"No. I just didn't realize how late it was. We're expanding the operation," she added for Samuel's benefit.

"Sounds like good news." Sammy pushed to his feet. "You two have business to discuss. I'll find Aidan and have him take me back to my car. We can finish our conversation later."

Moo stood when she did. She ruffled the dog's head.

"Yes. We're definitely not finished. I'm sorry I didn't look for you when we were in Guatemala. I am sorry for lots of things. I'll call you later."

"Right." Nodding, Samuel left. Her explanations had not erased the hurt on his face.

She glared at Brendan on her way to her bedroom to change. She plopped down on the bed, sick and tired of all the interruptions. Her life was supposed to be settled after she'd accepted Brendan's proposal. She stared at the glittering diamond. Her stomach churned as she thought of the simple gold band tucked away at the back of her jewelry case. The one Samuel had given her. She'd been sure when Brendan asked her to marry him.

She rubbed her eyes. Accepting his proposal had seemed the next step. Samuel's simple wedding ring a forgotten memory until now. But was it the right decision?

A sharp rap on the door had her jerking upright. "Are you decent?"

Before she could respond, Brendan walked through the door. "What happened with the preacher's kid? Did ya get him to sign?"

"We talked."

"'Tis a simple thing to do. Get him to sign the paper." A flash of annoyance darkened his face, sounded in his voice.

She wasn't going to apologize. "First, I need to understand what happened, why Samuel never came. And he deserves to know what happened to me."

Brendan's square jaw tightened. "You need to be hurrying. We don't want to be late for this meeting. The Guatemalan distributor is anxious to settle things."

"I'm ready. Let's go. We should see his operation before we sign. I'm sure Samuel would help us. He's lived there for years. He knows the place, the people."

Brendan's gaze sharpened as it met hers. "We don't need Fitzpatrick. We can go ourselves if you think you need to see the new place. I'm sure it's the same as the others."

"Then why do we even have to have this meeting? I don't want to go. I have a special order to finish." She glanced at her project.

A tense silence stretched between them. He walked toward her. His hands held her shoulders as his eyes met hers in a softened gaze. "Sure, and you do. You need to remember we'll be helping those women down there have a better life."

She wavered. Of course, she wanted to help. That had always been her goal. Making money didn't mean that much to her. "All right, I'll come with you to dinner but only if you promise we'll check out the operation in person. With Samuel."

His nod said yes, but his stiff neck contradicted the words.

Chapter 8

Sammy found Aidan in the chicken coup, collecting eggs. "Hey. When you finish can you take me back to my car?"

"You and Tiff through talking?"

"Brendan showed up."

Aidan glanced toward the farmhouse. "That's a shame. Be with ya in a minute. Just need to put these on the porch."

As they walked back to the farmhouse, Sammy could see Brendan and Tiff through the large picture window. Body language told him the conversation was more argument than discussion. His hope gauge rose a degree. He shouldn't like to see Tiff angry with the man she was planning to marry, but his gut told him she didn't belong with Brendan.

Aidan stuck his head inside the backdoor after he put the basket on the porch table. "I'll be taking Samuel to his car now."

Tiff appeared in the doorway. Her gaze met Sammy's. "I'll call as soon as our meeting's done."

"That'd be good." *Very good.* He followed Aidan.

Sammy opened the front door of the SUV sidestepping the back door Aidan held open. "Okay if I sit up here?"

"No worries." Aidan slid behind the wheel.

"Nice car. How long have you been with Tiff?"

"Almost ten years."

Sammy did the mental math. That meant Aidan started driving Tiff while she was still in art school. "Why did a student need a chauffeur?"

Aidan's knuckles flexed on the steering wheel. "That'd be a question for Tiffany. Ask me something else."

"Duly noted. Do you think she's happy?"

"Hmm." His fingers flexed up and out while his thumbs secured the wheel. "That's for her to say. Me, I'm thinking she was happier before Mr. Brendan improved her business and asked her to marry him." The word improved carried a tone of disgust.

"But her work's highly sought after. It sells well."

"Aye. True. Only that does not necessarily mean she's happy."

"She seems happy."

"Seems is not happy either." Aidan guided the car through Backwoods' parking area to Sammy's car and shoved the gear shift into park. Turning to him, he added, "She'd be smiling more today than since I met her."

"Are you saying she's not happy with Brendan? I thought she loved him."

"I think she wants to because of how he's helped her business when it was struggling. But go on... Fond, yes. Comfortable, maybe. Love, I don't think so."

"Why would she agree to marry him if she didn't love him?"

"She's thinking she owes him." Shadows crossed Aidan's face. "That's not love, that's gratitude. You don't say you love a man because he's grown your business. Especially when that man did it all because he fancied your business as much as you."

"Are you saying—"

"You go on now. I've said too much." Aidan shoved back against the seat and clutched the steering wheel.

Sammy opened the car door and stepped out. "Thanks for the ride and the discussion."

The gravel crunched beneath the tires as Aidan drove away. His conversation with Aidan pinged around in his head adding more questions to his already lengthy list. What if Aidan was right and Tiffany wasn't *in love* with Brendan? She'd agreed to marry him in a misplaced sense of gratitude. That possibility eased his conscious about pursuing an engaged woman. He wished one of his brothers was here to bounce things off.

When Sammy pulled into his parking space at the duplex, a man leaned into the open door of an unfamiliar vehicle in the driveway of the other duplex. He recognized the cleric collar on the black shirt when the man helped a woman out of his car. Sammy started toward them. The man stiffened and gave him a frown that said stay away.

With a defeated shrug, Sammy headed inside. There was a knock on his door a few minutes later. A man, the one he'd seen next door, stood with his hand extended. "Hi, I'm Chaplain Mike. Ava tried to reach you to let you know I'd be moving someone in but got no answer."

Sammy pulled his phone from his pocket. He'd put it on silent for his talk with Tiff. "Oops. I forgot to turn it back on. Anything I can do to help?" He needed something to take his mind off Tiff and their situation.

"For now, she's fine. The crisis neutralized. Ava will check on her later."

"What happened?"

"Not my story to tell." Chaplain Mike handed him his card. "Call me if you see anything suspicious."

"Sure. I know better than to ask. Wish I could offer to help but I'm waiting on a call. When it comes, I'll have to leave."

"That's fine. Ava's covering today."

"Didn't you do Faith and Blake's wedding?"

"I did. And you're one of the brothers who couldn't come."

"I stayed behind to mind Greenvine and let Josh and Mara attend."

"That's right." Mike's chin nodded. "Ava tells me you're here for a few weeks. Say, if you're looking for something to do, we could use an experienced volunteer. A unit's returned from overseas and that means things at the chapel pick up."

"Sure. Would tomorrow be okay?" If Sammy sat around doing nothing much longer, he'd go crazy.

"Great. We have afternoon appointments at the Post Chapel. There are always drop-ins. See you tomorrow."

"I'll be there." Sammy smiled. Helping families in Guatemala had always filled him with a sense of purpose. A part of him longed to return. But the mission board didn't seem to be in a hurry for him and other missionaries to return. Too unsettled there."

The afternoon grew eons long as Sammy waited and waited. Hours seemed like years, but no call came. Giving up, he showered and climbed into bed. He'd just closed his eyes when he heard shouting through the wall. He couldn't understand the words but the conversation was not friendly.

When there was a loud crash sound, Sammy quit debating with himself and pulled on jeans and a tee-shirt. Her front door was open. A car streaked down the street.

"Everything all right in here?" he called as he entered, not liking what he saw. Chairs were tipped on the floor and the wall next to the bedroom door had a fist hole. "Are you okay?"

The woman struggled to get to her feet. "I'm fine. Just not good with crutches."

Sammy extended his hand. She shoved it aside to brace her hand on the bed and heave her body up. "Who are you?"

"I'm Sammy Fitzpatrick. I'm staying next door."

"Kelsey Kelly. I know. Just call me KK everyone does. I didn't think Ava rented that side."

"It's only a temporary thing. Which do you prefer KK or Kelsey?"

"Kelsey."

"Then Kelsey it is. I'll get ice for your cheek."

The red blotch on her cheek was going to be a nasty bruise. Her eye would be swollen shut. He went to the kitchen. Broken glass littered the floor. Whatever went on hadn't been pleasant.

He held the ice tied in a dish towel to her cheek gently. "Sorry about the pointy edges. No peas. I had to improvise with crushed ice cubes."

"It's fine. I'm not much of a cook. Jax says I can't boil water."

"That's why God created take-out."

Her cheeks rose with a soft chuckle. She flinched. "Ouch."

"You want me to take you to the ER, let them check out your foot and eye, just in case?"

She shook her head and winced again. "No. I'll be okay."

"Maybe I should call someone? Chaplain Mike?"

"No, please. I can't cause more trouble for Jax."

If Jax did this, then someone needed to cause trouble for him Sammy thought but didn't give voice. "Then let me help you."

"That's not necessary."

"You need to lie down and get that foot elevated. What happened?" He reached around her and puffed the pillow at her back and grabbed a second pillow from the couch.

She scooted back against the headboard. "Originally, I tripped over Jax's rucksack. This time I dropped a glass and fell trying to pick up the pieces. Bad cook and klutz."

More likely Jax shoved you. Those bruises on your arms look a lot like handprints.

Sammy put the other pillow under her foot. "You rest while I straighten things up."

"You don't have to do that. I'll get to it later. Go back to your place and get some sleep."

"I wasn't sleeping much anyway. You have something for pain?"

"On the bathroom counter."

He came back with a glass of water and a couple of Extra Strength Tylenol. Kelsey tossed the pills down. "You can go now."

"I'll just make sure you're asleep." He backed out of the bedroom doorway.

By the time Sammy had the place in order and all the broken glass cleaned up, she was fast asleep. He stretched out on the couch and checked his phone. Still no call or text from Tiff.

Chapter 9

Tiffany's eyes popped open as morning sunbeams lit her bedroom and danced on her face. Dreams had wrestled with sleep all night and won. The rest she'd needed had eluded her. She pulled her knees to her chest and twisted and rolled her body like her physical therapist recommended. Stress and lack of sleep brought back the tightness, the aching.

She nestled beneath the covers again and closed her eyes hoping to grab another hour, but visions of Samuel's reddish-brown hair popped into her head. She'd always loved his thick, wavy hair with strands shooting here and there making him look like he'd just woken up. Their connection should have died after all this time. Being with him, looking into his sleepy blue eyes again, she felt sucked back in—all the feelings, the love, the hate, the emotions she'd shut down for the last ten years were resurfacing.

Did she even want to return to her past?

Yesterday's encouraging appointment with the financial backers secured a sound future for Fischer Textiles. Growth beyond anything she or Brendan could have ever imagined. The ability to aid countless women raised a thousandfold. That's where her focus should be. Samuel was her past. He had no place in her present or future.

Tossing the covers back, she clutched her grandmother's quilt to steady herself against the stiffness and limped toward the smell of fresh-brewed coffee. Moo bounded ahead, anxious for her breakfast.

"Good morning, *Mo cara*. Hard night?" The musical Irish lilt in Aidan's words made her smile.

She nodded.

"Not surprised. Yesterday was hard. A lot to be taking in."

When she'd left in-house rehab nine years ago, the hospital recommended Aidan as a personal trainer. He'd been with her ever since. At times, the way he read her mind, it was like he'd always been with her. He pulled out one of the pressed-back chairs circling the cross-sewn oak round table then set a mug in front of her. "Off to Backwoods or fresh eggs here?" He pointed to the full egg basket. "The hens were generous today."

"A fried egg would be heavenly."

Soon the aroma of bacon filled the kitchen and the sizzle of fresh egg dropping into the drippings followed. Tiffany watched through the screen door as sunlight pushed through the trees and danced with the baby goats. Tension between her shoulders lessened. The ache in her hips and lower back dulled until the toaster popped and pulled her back into the world of reality. She sipped her coffee as Aidan set her plate and a glass of orange juice in front of her. "What are ya about today?"

"I should call Samuel. I promised, but I was too tired when I got home from our bank meeting to continue our conversation." She scooped a bite of egg on her fork with the toast.

"Will you be calling him this morning? Finish your talk?"

"Maybe. Later. I need to get that special-order piece for Ms. Moore done. I told her I needed a month. It's already been three weeks, if I don't work on it today, I'll never finish on time."

"Work and talk. We do it all the time."

"Not this kind of talking." She finished off the last of the egg, laid her folded napkin beside her empty plate, and pushed from the table. "Thank you and thank the hens. Their eggs were delicious as always. Do you mind catching the home phone, please? I'm turning off my cell while I work. I don't want to be disturbed."

"I understand. No Brendan calls. No Samuel?" His eyebrow rose questioningly as he lifted her empty plate.

"No Samuel either. I will call him. Just not now."

She couldn't wrap her head around all that was happening and the confusing feelings about *her husband*. Maybe having him along on the trip to Guatemala would clear things up.

Or muddle things more, the voice in her heart whispered.

Brendan didn't want him along, but her name was on the company letterhead and she wanted Samuel's input. A part of her needed to see Samuel's world through his eyes, to understand why he'd chosen a missionary life over her.

Moo brushed gently against her knee as she stood. She either sensed her uneasiness and was reassuring her or simply herding her to the studio with her breed instinct. Either way, she squatted down to her level and scratched the dog's head with love, receiving a very wet kiss in return.

Samuel woke the next morning with leaden dread in the pit of his stomach. Deep down fear that Tiff wasn't going to call. For as long as he'd known her, s*he'd never been as comfortable with sharing personal thoughts and feelings as he had and this whole situation was a feelings doozey.*

At least for him. He'd give her another day then he'd insist they talk. Judge Hunt's ultimatum loomed like the Peanuts character Pig Pen's cloud of dust. It wasn't going away.

He slung the sheet off and trudged to the shower. As he toweled off, his phone rang. He dove across the bed to grab it.

"Hello."

"Sammy, it's Kelsey, next door. I need your help. Can you give me a ride to the chapel? My car won't start."

What was she thinking to drive in the first place? Her right foot was in a cast. "Sure. I'll be right over."

Kelsey met him at his car with a huge, overloaded tote in her hand along with the crutch grip. "Sorry to bother you, but Chaplain Mike said to call because you were coming to the chapel today anyway. You are still planning to go?"

"Uh-huh." And grabbing a coffee would be his first

order of business. "What about your car?"

"He's gonna send someone over to look at it."

"You shouldn't be driving with one foot and one eye anyway. What's in the bag?"

"Craft supplies for project day at the chapel." She handed it to him.

"Does everyone work on the same project?" he asked as he climbed behind the wheel.

"Oh no. We all do our own thing. What we make gets donated to various places."

"What are you working on?"

"Lap blankets and wall hangings. I use the chapel's quilting frames. Our quarters were never large enough for one."

"Sounds like someone else I know. Tiff has a whole room for her loom," Sammy said as he paused at the Ft. Bragg guard house. The guard waved him through, thanks to the special visitor pass Blake secured when he got tired of the calls from the guards to verify Sammy was legit.

"Who's Tiff?"

How did he answer? His wife once. Legally was now. But who she would be was still up for grabs. He whipped his Subaru Legacy into a handicap parking spot at the chapel entrance. He'd move it later. "It's not important."

Kelsey cut him a questioning frown. "Somehow I don't think that's true."

He reached for her tote. "Let me help."

"I can manage." Her bravado faded as they approached the door. She stopped and studied the ground.

"Did you forget something?"

"No. It's just I'm a little embarrassed. Last month my arm was in a sling."

"If you want to go back to the duplex, I'll take you."

"No." She squared her shoulders and reached for the door handle. Without another word, she waved Sammy away and walked straight to the quilting stand set up in a corner with her head held high.

The room was all set up and abuzz with voices. People sat at tables or in circles and worked on projects. He wasn't sure why Chaplain Mike thought he needed him.

He searched for the coffee and doughnuts table. There was always an obligatory refreshment table. A prerequisite for every church function. He'd grab a cup of coffee and then check in with Chaplain Mike. He found both at the coffee table. "Doesn't look like you need my help. Everything's set up."

Chaplain Mike chuckled. "And, as you know, it will all have to come down after. That's when you'll be handy to have around."

"Yep. The life of a preacher's kid. Setup and teardown."

"For now, why don't you walk around and visit?"

"Anyone, in particular, I should target?"

"Follow your instincts." Mike sipped his coffee and walked away.

Sammy stared after him, wishing for more guidance. This wasn't Greenvine or Guatemala. But then, people were people everywhere.

He wandered around watching nimble fingers craft jewelry, crochet needles clicking to form infant caps, and sewing machines hum stitching seams. Men and women sanded game boards while others painted chess board squares on them. Groups packed finished items into boxes labeled for shipment to various local locations and overseas FPOs and APOs.

Impressive operation and interesting people. He did wonder how many were in the same circumstances as Kelsey.

At noon, Mike announced lunch and the crafters tided up their work. The noise level rose with chatter as friends ate sandwiches and salads donated by the mess hall. Sammy drifted over to where Kelsey sat with an older woman he'd met earlier. "I'm hanging around to help Mike straighten up for the youth meeting tonight. Mind waiting around?"

"Not at all. I usually help." She raised a crutch. "Guess I get a hiatus."

"No reason to wait, dear. I'll be happy to drive you home." Ms. Patel patted her hand. "You need to get off that foot."

Kelsey studied her empty plate. "That's okay. I'll just wait for Sammy."

"There's no shame in being at the chaplain's sanctuary place, you know. Means you're a strong woman to get out of a bad situation." She squeezed Kelsey's hand. "I'll take you."

"Thank you."

Sammy gave an approving smile to Ms. Patel. "I'll come back to carry your stuff when it's time." Kelsey's tote was as big as the diminutive grey-haired woman and probably weighed as much.

"That would be lovely, son. Now I need to get back to

sanding." Ms. Patel slid her face mask band over her ear and disappeared.

Kelsey headed back to the quilting loom. Sammy checked his phone.

Chapter 10

At three o'clock, Chaplain Mike sounded the ending bell. Sammy went to help Kelsey to Ms. Patel's car. When he returned, Mike was collapsing folding tables. Sammy flipped the nearest table and did the same.

With the last table stored and all the chairs in a neat circle, Mike slapped a high five with Sammy. "Good having you here today. Come sit a spell in my office. You can tell me about that call you're waiting on."

Sammy cocked his head. "Faith put you up to this?"

"Nope. I watched you checking that phone of yours all day. Saw the disappointment on your face. Come on."

Coffee mug in hand, Mike waved him to the facing chairs in his small office space. "Faith did say you just found out the teenage marriage you thought had been annulled wasn't. And you're here for a divorce hearing. That's got to be tough. I'm available to listen."

Talking to Mike might help him make sense of things.

"Tough? That's an understatement. I've loved Tiffany Fischer for—" He shrugged. "All my life."

"That's not a bad thing. I see too many marriages where that's not the case."

"It is when you've been married to a woman for ten years and didn't know it. Then you find out she's a successful businesswoman engaged to a wealthy man."

Mike's eyebrows rose. "Whew. That *is* a hard one. Have you two chatted at all?"

"Briefly, yesterday. Her fiancé showed up and took her off to a business meeting. She said she'd call after."

"That explains all the phone checking."

Sammy lifted his phone and checked again. "She hasn't called."

"Day's not over yet. What's stopping you from calling her or going to see her?"

Sammy folded his hands prayer-like, braced his elbows on the chair arms, and dipped his head to rub his forehead. What *was* stopping him? Seconds ticked by before he raised his head. "I guess I don't know what I want to say or do."

"What are your options?"

"Not many. She's engaged. Even though she didn't know she was still married, that's a commitment. A vow. I should sign the divorce papers and walk away. But watching her with that man, I don't think she'll be happy with him. I'm afraid their marriage could become a Kelsey situation."

"And you want to see the woman you love happy."

Sammy nodded.

"Okay then, if our situations were reversed and you were talking to me, what would you tell me?"

He looked into Mike's eyes and said with utter honesty. "I don't know. It's so complicated."

Mike waited for him to continue. "Judge Hunt allowed

us only six weeks to decide what we want to do. Tiff has moved on, and I should let her get on with her life. But I have lots of unanswered questions."

"And you want those answers. Did you stop to think Tiffany might want answers too? She may have turned to the other guy because she thought you'd abandoned her."

Sammy rolled his shoulders, digesting that possibility. "What are you saying?"

"You need to know her side of the story. Do you know where she lives?"

He nodded.

"Then go see her. You're not asking her to come back to you. You're trying to get answers and free yourself, and her, to go on with your lives."

Sammy sat for a moment. He'd always want her back, but until he knew what had happened, he'd never find peace. He pushed from his chair. "You're right. Thank you."

On the walk to his car, Chaplain Mike's words burrowed around and through Sammy's head. Tiffany needed answers as much as he did. He hadn't considered that.

Relaxing for the first time since he'd received the divorce papers, he pulled his phone from his pocket to call her then shoved it back. No.

He'd go see her in person. That was better than phoning. On the way, he'd stop at that Backwoods place and grab milkshakes. Their hard discussions in the past had always gone better over milkshakes.

"Milkshake and conversation?" Sammy raised the carton

with two tall Styrofoam cups when Tiff opened the door.

For long moments memories danced between them, almost tangible. He could see them in her eyes, felt them in himself. He drew in a long breath and held it, steeling his heart against the thought that she could turn him away.

Slowly a familiar, welcoming smile spread across her face. She pushed the screen door open, stepped aside, and motioned for him to enter.

Moo bolted from behind her and nudged his elbow. The tray with the milkshakes tilted. Tiff grabbed Moo's collar. "Sorry, come in. Those are not for you," she scolded the dog.

He lifted the takeout tray above the dog's reach and followed her to her studio.

"I apologize for not calling yesterday. Our meeting went much longer than I expected. I was exhausted, and I had to work on this project for my client. I'm almost finished." She paused at her worktable.

Sammy stared at an abstract configuration of fabrics draped and bunched with jewelry pinned randomly on the quilt-like creation. The design stretched taut on a quilting rack like Kelsey had used.

"It's almost finished. I only have two more jewelry pieces to incorporate."

"Interesting. It's a cross between a quilt and a painting."

"The fabric and jewelry belonged to my client's grandmother."

"Nice way to remember a loved one."

"I agree. I do several special orders a year." Taking a

sip of her milkshake, she waved him to the other end of the room.

Minutes passed in *satiated silence. Sammy watched the sun setting through her picture window while he framed and reframed questions in his head.*

Tiff pushed her toe against the floor to give the hammock chair a tiny shove and spoke as though reading his thoughts. "You've told me how you couldn't find me. I need to explain... It's not a simple story. Or pretty. I'm not even sure where to begin." She lifted her head and met his gaze. "You have to believe I had no idea Daddy never filed the annulment papers. We never talked about it when they moved here. Or that Brendan had filed divorce papers. I'm always signing off on things he gives without reading thoroughly. It's a bad habit."

"Your daddy was dead set against our marriage. I just can't understand why he never filed the papers he made us sign."

"We'll never know now that he's gone." Her eyes filled and she blinked back the tears. She rubbed her bare foot along Moo's back. "Mostly, I think, his plans for me didn't fit with a preacher kid who talked about a career on the mission field."

"From where I'm sitting all his dreams for you came true."

"Remember, things are not always what they seem. Mom and I tried to convince him I could be married to a missionary and continue my art. He wouldn't listen."

"Your mom was always my biggest supporter. We should have told her what we were doing. She might have run interference."

"Probably. She's the one who convinced Dad to let me go to school in North Carolina in the first place."

"But they followed you. What was that all about?"

"Disaster after disaster." Combing her fingers through the mass of fur on Moo's head, she stood. "Finished?"

Sammy circled the straw around the bottom of the cup sucking up every drop of milkshake before he closed his hand over hers as he handed the container to her. His thumb rubbed slowly over her knuckles. She tried to draw her hand away, but his grasp tightened. "I've never stopped loving you, you know. I need to understand… we both do."

She held on another second longer. The pulse in her neck surged before she turned and walked away.

A frown wrinkled her forehead when she returned. She went to the mantel and stared at the family pictures. "My life looks perfect. Like all Daddy planned for me happened, all I ever dreamed came true. But it's not what it seems." Too much happened after she'd left Samuel at that bus terminal. "You remember how controlling Daddy was… in by 9 p.m., you're not leaving this house in those clothes, not that movie. When I got to Chapel Hill, I thought I'd escaped."

"Escaped what, my Luv?" Brendan walked into the room.

She whipped around. "What are you doing here? I left a message I'd be staying at the farm tonight. Didn't you get it?"

"I did. I was wanting to be sure…" He noticed Sammy. "What are you doing here?"

She took Brendan's hand and tugged him toward the front door with Moo close at her side. "We're talking. You need to go back to town and let us."

"But—" He planted his feet.

"No. This is between Samuel and me. You need to leave."

For a long moment, the three of them simply stared at each other. Aidan appeared behind her. "What are you at here, Mate?"

"Nothing. I'm leaving," Brendan growled.

"Good then, I'll go with you." Aidan opened the front door. "We'll grab a pint."

Brendan fired one last glare at Samuel then back at her. "I'll call you in the morning."

Chapter 11

Sammy couldn't make himself look away no matter how uncomfortable and awkward the scene playing out before him. He struggled to read the dynamics, to understand the subtext, and know if there was more going on than his presence. His recent encounter with Kelsey made him wonder if Brendan held some spell over Tiff.

She returned to her studio room. Her smile did not reach her eyes. "Sorry about that. Brendan sometimes..." her voice trailed off. "It's not important. Would you like something to drink?"

"No thanks. I'm still full of the milkshake." Was Brendan physically abusive as well as overly possessive? He needed to know and took the direct approach. "Brendan's not abusive, is he?

"Heaven's no. Self-centered. Yes, but no way he'd ever hurt me."

"Why did Aidan come running?"

"Because he's Aidan. He sees himself as my self-appointed champion and defender."

That answer only muddied the water more. "Do you need a champion and defender?"

"Not really. Not anymore. Except for his driving. I'll always need a driver."

"What do you mean?"

"Let me finish my story and you'll understand." She curled into the rattan hammock chair. "After I left you, I was on my own for the first time ever. Daddy wasn't watching my every move. I was free, and I knew you'd be coming for me. Sadly, I didn't manage all that freedom well. By the middle of the semester, Mom and Dad had moved to Chapel Hill and insisted I live at home."

"But didn't your scholarship cover room and board?"

"If I'd kept my grades up. I was failing everything except my art classes. The college let them know and that's when they showed up."

"You stopped answering my letters. Why?"

"I never got any from you after I moved home. Dad must have intercepted them."

"That would be no surprise. He never liked me."

"But I never found any letters when I shut down the house after the accident either."

"He probably burned them. What accident?"

"The one where I killed my parents."

Sammy shook his head. *That couldn't be.* "I'm sure you didn't kill your parents. What happened?"

Tiff rose and walked to the fireplace. For long minutes she stared at the picture of her parents then gripped the mantel and rested her forehead on her hands. "Living at home was hard. I felt like a prisoner. My art was all I had."

She raised her head and walked to stand over her loom. Her hand lovingly caressed the piece she showed him earlier. "I started entering my stuff in juried shows and won, even began to sell pieces. That's when Dad decided I didn't need a degree and should drop out of school and focus on creating and selling things. We built a following by entering lots of shows all over the country. And that's when it happened." She sank to her work stool to face him. Her voice so lifeless it was frightening. He battled the urge to curl her into his arms and cocoon her from the painful memories.

"We were on the way home from an art show. I hadn't sold as much as we'd wanted. It poured down rain all day and the crowds had been slim. We were all short-tempered. Having to wait our turn under the porte-cochere to load our small trailer for the trip home only added more frustration. We loaded the trailer and argued over who should drive. Dad insisted. He didn't trust my driving in the rain."

Tiff pinched her eyes closed, sucked her lips between her teeth, and swallowed before going on, "After we'd been on the narrow two-lane road for a while, he asked me if I'd remembered to pack his toolbox. I hadn't. I'd left it in the space we'd rented. Mom reminded him it was *his* toolbox he should have loaded it himself. He whipped his head around to yell at her. A flash of lights lit the interior of the car.

Mom screamed.

Dad swerved to avoid the eighteen-wheeler hydroplaning into us. But our little trailer jackknifed us into the cab. The front seat took the full brunt of the impact. They didn't stand a chance."

When her eyes opened her hazelnut irises had crystalized into a deep, dark grey, the color of the sky above Greenvine's lake when storm clouds gathered. Her pupils grew large until her eyes appeared black. She covered her face. Moo licked at the back of her hands. "It was my fault. If I hadn't forgotten his toolbox... I should have been driving..."

In a heartbeat, Sammy leaped from his chair to kneel in front of her. His hands rested on her knees. "It was an accident. It wasn't your fault."

"I know that. In here." She tapped her temple. Her hand slid down to press against her heart. "But in here I can never forgive myself. I'll never drive again."

No point to argue with her. He'd never convince her. But knowing about the accident helped answers fall into place like pieces of a puzzle. "That's how you met Aidan?"

"I spent months in hospitals and rehab. He was one of the nurse practitioners on my case. I don't think I'd be walking if Aidan hadn't pushed me and encouraged me. I had no one else."

"I would have come."

"I did call your family. They told me you were in Guatemala doing the mission work you'd always dreamed of. I wasn't sure I would ever get out of that wheelchair. I couldn't ask you to come home and be saddled with a cripple. Better for you to find someone else. Someone whole."

"None of that would have mattered." Sammy pulled her to her feet and into his arms. Having her in his arms felt right, perfect... like only yesterday, not the lifetime that had passed. Resting his chin on her head, her never forgotten scent, clean with a hint of flowers from her shampoo, hung in the air filling him with an intense longing that had never dimmed. "I loved you. I'll always love you."

She looked up. Before he could think of all the reasons he shouldn't, his mouth lowered to hers. The second their lips touched, all the emotion he'd been trying to control exploded into one colossal, amazing kiss. He never wanted to stop. This was what he'd secretly longed for since he'd first seen her at the fair. This was where she belonged—in his arms, her lips on his. His control dissolved. He pulled her tighter to his body, deepened the kiss. Her soft clinging body went stiff. Her forehead sank onto his chin.

"We can't do this," she muttered against his chest.

Her whispered tone and her arms still squeezing his body might deny what she said but the realization of what he'd done slammed him full force. He'd only meant it to be a simple kiss, no more than a comforting peck to ease the hurt and pain he'd heard as she described the accident. He took a deep breath and unclasped her arms from around his waist, and, ignoring how right it might feel, how right it was, he forced himself to step back.

Her words stung as much now as they had prom night. He'd tried to kiss away her pain and hurt that night too. She and her dad had fought over the short red cocktail dress she wore. The one she'd saved for and bought with her own money. Her father's angry words had destroyed her joy and happiness. One kiss led to another. They'd made out at every stoplight and stop sign along the way to the high school gym. After he'd pulled into the parking space, he'd wanted to scramble into the backseat.

"Not now," she'd said with a smile full of promise. "At least not until everyone's seen my dress."

He'd swallowed his libido. Just now, again, she'd stopped them from rushing into something. "You're right. I apologize for kissing you. You're engaged to someone else."

"Don't apologize. You weren't kissing by yourself. I kissed you back." She turned away. "I don't mean to send mixed signals. Seeing you again, learning we're still married, it's confusing. I thought I had my life all figured out. Everything's gone topsy-turvy."

"I'm trying to understand too."

"I know. It's complicated. Brendan is—" She rubbed her eyes. "I don't want to hurt either of you."

"I'll sign the divorce papers. I don't want to, but I will. All you have to do is tell me that's what you want." His heart was breaking with every word.

"No... I don't want you to sign..." She shook her head. "I don't know..." She rolled her shoulders. "I need more time."

He closed his hands around her forearms lightly and pressed his lips to her forehead in a soft, tender kiss. "It's okay. We'll figure this out."

Tiff wrapped her arms around him and returned a comforting squeeze. Sammy sank into her comfort

"Thanks," she said when she lifted her head. "Right now, I am starving. I didn't stop for lunch. Could I interest you in an omelet?"

The giant loss he felt as she slid from his arms nearly crumbled him. He wanted this connection to her, to her love, to her life. But he needed to be patient. "As a matter of fact, the ridiculously small salad I had at the Ft. Bragg Chapel with a room full of crafters has long disappeared and that milkshake was barely a filler. Did Aidan leave today's eggs on the porch table?"

Nodding, she went to the kitchen and began pulling cheese and mushrooms and spinach from the refrigerator. He headed for the eggs.

"What were you doing with crafters on the post? You don't do crafts." She peeked around the refrigerator door. "Or have you started?"

He set the basket on the counter beside her. "Heavens no. Crafts are not my thing. I took my new neighbor from the duplex. She's a quilter."

"Hmm. What's her name? I might know her. I know lots of quilters in the area."

"Kelsey Kelly."

"Her nickname KK?"

He watched Tiff drop butter into the omelet skillet then pour in the eggs. "She prefers Kelsey."

"I think I met her at a quilters meeting. She's good."

"All of them were. Some crocheted infant hats and blankets. Others sewed stuff like we always had at the church bazaar. Men were there too. Some knitting and crocheting and others gluing wooden toys."

"What happens to the finished products?" She sprinkled spinach over the mushrooms and cheese.

"Some of the things they ship to overseas orphanages and shelters, and some are sold at the post thrift store and local craft fairs."

"Interesting." Tiff set the omelets on the table and reached for his hand. "Will you say the blessing please?"

He did and lifted his head to find her watching him with a smile on her face. "I remember all the lunches with your family at the farm. You sounded just like Pastor Fitz." She lifted her fork and scooped up a bite of omelet.

Their conversation centered on the crazy things they'd done as teenagers as they ate. She asked about his siblings and kept circling back with questions about the crafters. "You think any of them might be interested in collaborating with me?"

He didn't know if Kelsey was looking for work. "Wouldn't hurt to ask. Kelsey might be. Why don't you come along with me next time and you two can talk?"

"Wonderful." Tiff stood to take the dishes to the sink.

There was a tap at the door and Aidan walked in. "Oi and isn't this a fine little domestic scene? I saw the kitchen light on and thought I'd best be checking."

"Is Brendan with you?" Worry laced Tiff's words.

"Nay. Pub owner put him in the cab." Aidan winked. "For an Irishman, he can't hold his. A few pints and he's a goner. And how are things here? Brilliant from the looks on your faces."

Tiff blushed. "We've talked. We're taking a break."

Sammy stood. "Tiff needs to finish her project. I'm heading out."

Aidan gave a thumbs up. "I'll go with ya."

Chapter 12

Sammy matched Aidan's steps to the backyard gate that led to his apartment. "Tiff shared about the car accident today. Thank you for looking after her. I wish I had been here. I *should* have been here. I wish I'd never stopped looking for her."

Aidan shrugged. "'If wishes were horses, beggars would ride,' as me Granny Mary always says. You're here now. That's a good thing."

"I'm afraid it's too late." Although the way she'd kissed him, he did wonder.

"Because of the ring?"

"It is an engagement ring. She's gonna marry him." *Which is why you shouldn't read too much into that kiss.*

"But she hasn't. No wedding planned yet either. 'Tis Brendan who's pushing."

A bit more encouragement settled in Sammy's chest. "How long has she had his ring?"

"Two years."

"What's stopping her?"

"Her heart."

Sammy stared at him. "Tiff said you and Brendan were friends."

"Brendan claims we're related. Some great-great grandma on my pa's side or some such. Me, I'll not be claiming blood with him."

"You're not sounding much like his friend either. Why'd you introduce him to Tiff?"

"Not my proudest moment."

"What do you mean?"

"I introduced them thinking he could help with her business. He's always about the business. I never expected him to ask Tiffany to marry him. Or her to say yes. He's not husband material. Not for her."

"You saying he doesn't love her?"

"That'd be something you'd best ask him." With that, he disappeared through the gate.

Sammy stuffed his hands deep in his pockets and looked back toward the house. She seemed content. Happy with her work. But was she?

Tiffany placed her palms against the counter and stiff-armed herself up to peer out the kitchen sink window. Sammy and Aidan talked as they walked together. They stopped at the back gate to Aidan's apartment. Too far away for her to hear anything. She slid back to the floor and loaded the dishwasher, taking one last peek as she flipped off the light over the sink. They were still talking.

What did those two have to talk about?

The memory of Sammy's kiss tingled on her lips as she went into her studio to finish her project. Lingering emotions sent vivid snapshots of her and Samuel together began to cascade through her head. Their first kiss stolen on the playground in fifth grade when no one was watching. More a bumping of closed lips than a true kiss. The necking sessions in the church balcony while their moms worked in the kitchen. Those had carried more skill. By senior year, the kisses were movie worthy. She fingered her lips.

Brendan's kisses never felt like that.

Cupping the back of her neck, she rubbed, trying to shake off her mood, then picked up the box of jewelry her client had left. Rings and pendants and clip earrings shifted in the wooden box. A vintage Victorian pin caught her eye. Cast of triple plate silver over copper, the reddish metal showed through in worn places. Two interlocking hearts with initials engraved where they overlapped.

The flourished letters in an Old English font looked like her and Samuel's initials. Her heart pounded against her chest as a memory of the carving tree on the island at Greenvine church camp floated in her head. Every teenager who ever attended carved initials of their summer love. Faith and Blake. Josh and Mara. Samuel's oldest brother Caleb and Carrie had been one of the first. One summer she and Samuel had added theirs.

She pulled her magnifying glass from the jar of pencils and pens and looked at the pen closer. The swirls weren't TF and SF like hers and Samuel but IS and CS her client's grandparents.

The piece would be a marvelous focal point. Positioning it in various places, she finally settled on the perfect spot and sewed the pin into place with a fancy embroidery stitch. Propping the finished wall hanging on the display shelf, she admired the final creation. Her client would be pleased.

Moo pawed at her leg ready to head to bed. She glanced at the time. "Oh my, you're right, girl. It's way past our bedtime."

Her phone rang as she stood beneath the starlit sky with the dog. "Brendan?"

"Tiffany, tell me he's gone?" His words slurred. He drank a lot when they first met but stopped when she'd asked. Samuel's return was messing with him as much as her.

"It's nearly midnight, Samuel left long ago. Go to bed, Brendan." She pressed end then waved for Moo to come. "Nighty, nighttime, girl."

Moo hopped on the bed while she showered. She pushed the big dog to the other side and climbed beneath the sheets. An hour later, she was still flipping her pillow and adjusting covers. Her conversation with Samuel about the accident wouldn't stop playing in her mind.

It's not the accident and you know it. Samuel had stirred her heart.

Learning she was still legally married amplified her doubts about a life with Brendan. She'd been putting Brendan off for years. She did love him though not the way she'd loved Samuel.

Brendan didn't want children claiming he was far too old to deal with diapers and teens. That was a major stumbling block. One she thought she could live with. Until now.

If only there were a simple, easy answer. How did

she return Brendan's ring and keep their business partnership? It'd be too hard and awkward. And she wasn't giving up her business.

Moo stood and licked her chin then plopped down with her paw on Tiff's chest as if to say, *go to sleep*. Tiff squeezed her eyes closed. Just as sleep settled, she stiffened and her eyelids popped open again. She hadn't mentioned the Guatemala trip to Samuel.

Chapter 13

Sammy spotted large, striped umbrellas at the fashionable downtown Fayette eatery where Brendan said they'd meet when he called earlier. According to the sign the trendy place that served dishes prepared with local ingredients and brews from North Carolina seemed more like someplace that would appeal more to Tiff than Brendan. The crisp feel of fall took the edge off the lingering summer they'd been having. He opted for a table outside.

In the early morning call Brendan said he had business to discuss. What did he mean by *business*? Unless Brendan counted Tiff as a business.

Sammy certainly didn't. After hearing about her accident and her inability to get behind the wheel because of it, he'd wanted to jerk that engagement ring off her finger and demand his wife come home with him.

That wasn't business. That was love.

A server with thin buzz-shaved hair and a chin-strap beard greeted him. "What can I get you, sir?"

"Iced tea, please. There'll be someone else joining me. We'll order then."

As his iced tea arrived, Tiff's car pulled up to the curb. He hadn't expected her. Only Brendan. Aidan hopped out to open her door with a wave and a wink to Sammy.

She stepped out wearing a long-woven skirt in brilliant colors of purple and orange and turquoise that she'd probably made herself and a bright, burnt-orange sweater. Large sunglasses with tortoise frames hid her eyes. Her hair fell softly at her shoulders. Brushing a wisp from her cheek, she removed the glasses and dropped them into the tote-size bag on her arm. When she looked up, their eyes met. Hers were soft and clear. The hazel orbs glittered in the sunlight. A soft smile curved her cheeks. The way she used to look at him.

His pulse scrambled. His throat went dry.

"Hi, Samuel," she said, joining him at the table. The sound of his name coming from her lips sent a mix of pleasure and anxiety through him.

"I thought only Brendan and I were meeting. I didn't know you would be joining us." His voice came out weak. Swallowing, he pulled out her chair. "Where is he?"

"Running late. His overindulgence at the pub last night got to him." Her tone said she wasn't happy about it either. Sammy couldn't tell which upset her more, the tardiness or the night at the pub.

The young server returned with Sammy's iced tea and a water. "I'll take your order when you're ready."

"Great. Turns out there'll be one more guest."

"I'll watch."

"Is Brendan late often?" Sammy paused hesitating to voice his next question, but he needed to know. Images of Kelsey were too vivid. "Or go on Guinness binges?"

"Tardiness, rarely. Drinking, not much anymore." Her voice trailed off as she sipped her water.

"Sorry. None of my business."

"No. It's a fair question. Finding out we're still married has shaken us all. We have different ways of coping." Her gaze met his. "But the divorce isn't the reason we're meeting. We're planning to produce a new line of landscape textiles. Brendan found someone with a shop in Guatemala and he wants me to go with him to have a look. I'd like for you to join us."

"Tiff, I'm not sure—"

Brendan arrived and kissed Tiff's cheek. "My apologies, Luv. Have you ordered?"

Sammy signaled their server. "Not yet."

After handing menus to the newly seated guests at another table, the server made his way to theirs. "Ready to order?"

"Yes," Sammy answered and picked up the menu.

Brendan pushed it down. "No need for the menu. We'll have the squash dip, an order of fried green tomatoes, and those southern eggrolls. Tiffany's favorites." He flashed a possessive smile at her then shifted a haughty look Sammy's way. "That work for you?"

"Sounds good. And more sweet tea for me," he added.

Tiff chuckled, a soft, knowing laugh. "Samuel always drank sweet tea like it was water."

"I can't seem to break the habit."

Brendan squeezed Tiff's hand. "See, Luv, I'm not the only one with bad habits."

Sammy wasn't sure Guinness and sweet tea were in the same league.

"Habits are not easy to break. I'm not without my own hang-ups." Her gaze drifted to her parked car. "But we're not here to discuss bad habits. Tell us about Guatemala, Samuel."

"Sure. What do you want to know?"

"Brendan met a South Korean with a textile factory there. We thought we'd go check it out and get you to come along."

"That's not a good idea." Samuel took a deep breath. "It's not safe there."

"What do you mean?"

"Says who?" Brendan demanded.

"The U.S. States Department. They told the missionaries to leave. That's why I'm home. Violence is a real problem because of the drug traders and human trafficking."

"All the more reason to bring work to help them. Right, Tiffany?" Brendan's voice was more declarative than questioning.

"I guess, but we shouldn't go if it's dangerous." She cut her eyes toward Sammy for confirmation.

"The people do need jobs. But you have to understand how unsettled it is there. Robberies happen all the time, especially in the mountains. It's not a place you should go."

Brendan let out a loud snort. "Fine, then Samuel and I can go."

"No." Tiff shook her head. "Y'all shouldn't go either."

"It might not matter what you want. Getting a visa won't be easy," Sammy said.

"Mr. Choi can get us in."

"Choi? Ha-Kun?" Sammy tamped down the concern rising like a volcano and leveled his voice. "He's who you're working with?"

"Do you know him?" Tiff's eyebrow rose as concern wrinkled her forehead.

"Not personally. But I know of him. He runs one of the larger *maquila*, a garment or textiles factory. His plants are dirty and unsanitary with poor ventilation and lighting. There's no drinking water. I don't think you want to work with him."

Tiff's eyes widened. Brendan rested his hand over hers. "We'll demand he fix them before we sign the agreement."

"Good luck with that. His word means nothing. Besides, you won't be there to ensure he complies."

Brendan's chest rose. Frustration hissed from his nostrils. "I'll hire someone who will be."

Sammy shrugged again. "It may not make any difference. He pays well and these people have nothing. What he offers entices them. Then he works them ten, twelve, or even more hours per day, with no overtime paid. No breaks, and the women, some as young as eight and ten, have no access to toilets except at certain times. The workers would come to the mission when they couldn't take anymore."

Because all the color had drained from Tiff's face, Sammy didn't add how the women were verbally abused, threatened, and sometimes beaten when they didn't meet quotas. They were humiliated, sexually harassed, and some even raped. "I can't tell you how many escaped to the mission for refuge."

Tiff pushed back, her shoulders stiff. "Brendan, you can tell Mr. Choi we are not interested." Determination and demand laced her words.

"We've signed a letter of intent. We can't be backing out—" the server arrived with their order interrupting Brendan's response.

"Bon appétit." He set the dishes in the center of the table and slid plates to everyone's place then, giving a barely perceptible bow, disappeared.

Tension simmered, the fourth guest at the table. Brendan lifted the fried green tomato platter to Tiff. Sammy served himself a spoonful of squash dip. For long minutes, the only voices were those coming from people seated around them.

Guatemala didn't come up again. But Sammy got the feeling it wasn't a dead topic between Tiff and Brendan. The frown never completely left his forehead. Their conversation turned to neutral topics—things to see in Fayetteville, books, and movies.

Their server reappeared. "Dessert?"

"Not for me. I have a client project to deliver." Tiff pulled her phone from her purse. "I'll let Aidan know we're finished."

"None for me either." Sammy shook his head.

"Another iced tea?" Brendan asked, but his tone suggested no choice. "We need to talk more."

"Sure," Sammy answered, wondering what he was getting into.

Aidan pulled Tiff's SUV to the curb. Brendan slid her chair from the table. He kissed her on the lips. "We'll talk more later."

"Thank you for telling us about Guatemala and Mr. Choi, Samuel. I want to find something I can do to help those women. We'll talk more about what and how." She squeezed him, whispering softly. "And discuss our situation more."

Her words and the feel of her arms around him shot reassuring waves of optimism through him. He wrapped her closer. Seconds stretched into minutes. Until Brendan cleared his throat, and they sprang apart.

With a deadly glare at Sammy, Brendan placed his arm snuggly at the small of her back and walked her to the car. He returned to the table in long, swift strides. "I'll not be having you messing me about with Tiffany or our business. I don't care what Mr. Choi has done in the past. We are expanding Tiffany's business and we need his *maquila*."

Sammy met Brendan's scowl square on. He clenched his back jaw until he thought his teeth would crack. "It is not safe, but I'm not stopping you from going. What I don't understand is why you don't use workers here in the U.S."

"Too expensive. Our profits would decrease."

Interesting. Brendan's focus was profits while Tiff cared about making life better for her workers. That must put stress on their business relationship.

"I'm not claiming to know how to run a business. But I'm quite sure there are women, and men, here in the area who would love to create those landscapes for her."

"Give it over. Exactly what are you after here?"

My wife, he wanted to shout. With other guests around, this was not the place to air dirty linen. "Certainly not your business. But I know Tiff and it would kill her to learn what she sells comes from sweathouses. Or God forbid she see a *maquila* like Choi's in person."

"She'll never know. I manage the business. She does the creative stuff. You need to be signing the divorce papers and move on." He reached into his jacket pocket, pulled out the folded papers, and slammed them on the table.

Sammy pushed them back at him. Brendan's cheeks turned red. "She'll be marrying me. Can't ya see the lass loves me?"

"If that's true, all she has to do is tell me, then I'll gladly sign the papers." As he shoved from the table, he added, "She hasn't and until she does, I won't sign anything. We're finished here."

Chapter 14

"How'd the meeting go?" Aidan asked as he started the car.

"Not good."

His eyes met hers in the rearview mirror. "Sure, and did you expect any different when you set up a meeting with your husband and your fiancé?"

Her shoulders rose in a sigh and sank in a shrug. "I know. Not a surprise. It was like watching two dogs eyeing a bone. Only I was the bone."

"The clock is ticking. You'll be needing to give a decision to the judge."

"I know. But this was more than that. Sammy knows the man Brendan wants to partner with in Guatemala. He runs a *sweatshop*. I'm not about to sign an agreement with him."

Aidan shook his head. "Brendan's about the money for sure, but he wouldn't be doing that. I don't believe it."

"Samuel doesn't lie."

Brendan? Well, she wasn't sure. Not after discovering he knew about the unsigned annulment papers and never told her. He wasn't forthcoming about business things, either. Not intentionally, she didn't think. He protected her from details to let her full focus be on creating new products. Same as her Dad had managed all the business stuff when she'd first started.

She hated doing paperwork. It made sense to hand the business stuff over to Brendan when they formed their partnership. She leaned her head on the headrest and stared through her side window at the cars zipping by.

She shouldn't have. She should give him the benefit of the doubt like Aidan when he introduced them. But she was beginning to have doubts.

Several of their mass-production factories were overseas. She wasn't even sure where or what each produced. Were they sweatshops too? She shivered at the possibility.

Aidan turned off the main road into one of the newer housing developments near the Fayetteville airport. Her client's sprawling, red brick house had a massive yard and a three-car garage.

"Lovely it is. You'd be needing to bring Brendan next time. Let him see," Aidan said as Tiff stepped out.

"Nope. His house is as big without the circular drive. He sees that and he'll be adding one."

Aidan chuckled. "That he would."

The sad thing was both places looked impressive but not inviting. Nothing that made a house look like a home to her. No evidence of children or a dog running around. Everything prim and proper.

She took the package Aidan lifted from the trunk. "I'm not planning to be long. Say an hour."

He walked her to the door carrying the box of unused jewelry. "I brought me iPad. I'll read while I'm waiting."

Forty-five minutes later, she said goodbye to a smiling Ms. Moore at the front door. "It's far more than I ever dreamed. I can't wait to see what you do with the picture. Thank you."

Aidan helped her into the car. "Sure, and she seems pleased."

"She was. I expect there'll be more orders after she shows her friends."

Tiffany would never tire of the personal relationship with her clients. It was the best part of what she did. The word-of-mouth promotion helped too.

She took out the photo Ms. Moore had given her. Her mother's colonial homestead with blooming crape myrtles along the driveway. Tall white columns framed the porch with wicker rockers and a small balcony with double French doors crowned the massive entrance. Ms. Moore's childhood home. She wanted another textile creation of it to display alongside her mother's jewelry. These were the projects Tiff enjoyed the most. Not producing ideas for mass production.

That had never been her plan. She'd agreed to Brendan's idea because it would mean more work for women in need. The women she hired worked from home and could never produce the volume a dedicated factory workshop could. That's why she'd let Brendan find the factories. But she'd never dreamed they'd be sweatshops. How could he even consider working with someone who ran one?

That he would made her wonder again about

the other factories Fischer Textile used. Were they sweatshops too? She had to know for sure. Asking him outright might not get an honest response.

"Aidan, I need you to do something for me."

"Whatever you're needing."

"Can you get a list of all our factories—locations, and what they make? I don't want Brendan to know I'm asking."

He glanced back with a questioning expression on his face. "Ah, I will."

"I have to be sure we're not using sweatshops," she answered the unasked question.

Sammy sat on Blake and Faith's small patio beside the metal garden dragon she'd bought at the craft fair. The weird, rusty creature looked like he belonged next to the brilliant red pot of geraniums. He rubbed his hand on his cheek. Had that only been three weeks ago? Seemed like a million years.

He hadn't heard a word from Tiffany since their meeting about Guatemala a week ago. No call. No text. Nothing.

He couldn't figure out what was going on. He'd thought they were making progress. He should be satisfied she hadn't asked him to sign the decree and be patient.

His phone vibrated in his pocket. The aluminum folding chair nearly toppled as he hurriedly dug his phone out. Only to discover the call was from his mom. "Hi, Mom. How are things in Texas?"

"Cooling off, finally. Our September summer may be ending. How are you?"

"Okay, I guess." His heavy sigh carried through the phone. "Tiff hasn't asked me to sign the papers. Or told me not to. That's positive."

"Aw, honey. I'm sorry it's not working out as you'd hoped. Are you coming home?"

"We have a couple more weeks until the judge's deadline, but I'm thinking about it. I'll let you know."

"It will work out. We know who's in control. I'll be praying." With more good wishes, she hung up.

Sammy filed her words along with the other reassurances he'd received. Kelsey's, "If that Brendan is running sweatshops, she's not gonna let him hang around."

Faith's, "You two had too much going for you. She'll remember and come back to you."

And Blake's, "She hasn't asked you to sign the papers yet. That's positive."

All meant to encourage him, but discouragement hung like a rusty, ship anchor around his neck.

"Cheer up." Faith slapped his feet off the chair across from him and sat.

"Why doesn't she call or answer mine?" Doubts pressed on him. "I should just sign the decree and go home."

"No. You won't," Faith said. "Lawyers have long believed the longer a jury deliberates, the better the chances of an acquittal. I'm thinking Tiffany's deliberating and her final decision will be in your favor."

Blake shifted in his chair. "You can't give up

especially considering Brendan's stand on the supplier in Guatemala and that supplier's sweatshop. She'll have to resolve that."

"Maybe you should go see her again," Faith said.

Sammy rubbed his hands down his pants legs. "I don't want to pressure her. This time I need to be patient, let her lead."

"Then come with me tomorrow. I'm doing a talk on legal separation for Mike's group. You can help with individual counseling."

"Sure." Listening to others' troubles would take his mind off his.

Chapter 15

Sammy bid farewell to the couple he'd been counseling with and followed the sound of laughter to the room where Faith had given her presentation. She must have told a joke because he didn't think divorce and separation were anything to laugh about. At least not from his experience.

Kelsey stood in the group of attendees talking with his sister. He worried about her. Her arms were still a brownish purple, but Sammy hadn't seen her husband Jax come around again. He hoped she'd listened to what Faith presented.

"Hey, little brother, how'd you do?" Faith asked.

"Think I helped. At least, they were talking as they left."

Kelsey took a step backward. "You're a marriage counselor? You didn't tell me that."

"No, no. The mission field is my job. Seminary training includes counseling courses and Chaplain Mike asked me to help today."

"He does give great advice." Faith slid her arm around his shoulder and squeezed. "He's the reason Blake and I are together."

Plenty of good advice for others. Why was it he still couldn't decide whether to sign those divorce papers?

"We ready to head out?" he asked. He and Kelsey had picked Faith up on the way to the chapel.

"Just let me tell Chaplain Mike goodbye. Meet you at the car."

"What'd you think of Faith's talk?" Sammy asked as he walked with Kelsey to the door.

"Everything she said made sense. But."

"But what? He should think about leaving Jax."

"How would I support myself? I've no training and, according to Jax I'm not capable of anything."

"Don't listen to Jax. Mike has a list of available training sessions in dozens of career areas."

"I'll think about it." She handed him her crutches and slid into the front seat.

After he dropped Faith off and had Kelsey settled next door, Sammy sat with a glass of fresh-brewed iced tea and stared at the divorce papers Brendan had shoved in his face last week. If only he felt confident in which way to turn.

A tap sounded at his door. He opened it expecting Kelsey who sometimes popped over for a chat.

It wasn't.

Backlit against the setting sun, Tiff smiled at him. Light slid in and out of her blond hair floating loosely at her shoulders. She stood close enough the lemony scent of her shampoo blended with the delicate fragrance of her perfume filling his nostrils with every breath. He braced himself for the rush of his pulse that accelerated whenever she was this close.

"Hi," she said. "I thought we'd continue our talk here, if that's okay."

He watched her lips move, but it took a few seconds to process her words. *Get a grip, Sammy. She just wants to talk.*

"Sure, come in."

"Brendan isn't likely to interrupt here."

"Right. How'd you get my address?" Dumb question. What did it matter? He was behaving like a teenager whose crush spoke to him in the cafeteria. *Focus, man.*

"Chaplain Mike. I'd have called Faith but I don't have her contact information. I hope it's okay."

"Sure. Absolutely. Have a seat." He scooped the divorce papers from the coffee table and carried them to the kitchen counter. "Can I get you something to drink? Iced tea is fresh."

"I'm good." She sat on the couch. Her pose relaxed. Her lips curved in a genuine smile. He couldn't shake the feeling her presence was not a good omen.

His return to the living area from the kitchen felt like a cross-country hike. He sat at the opposite end of the couch searching for any hints of why she'd come. Finding none, but fearing the worst, he lifted his chin. "I should start and explain why I never —"

"It's not a blame game, Samuel. Whatever your reasons, they're as valid as mine. But the whys don't really matter. I feel like we can be friends again once we both understand what happened."

Panic settled over him snuffing out his joy at seeing her. *This was it. She'd come to ask him to sign the divorce papers. The end.*

He couldn't breathe. He ran a hand through his hair and swallowed once, twice, to fish his voice from down between his toes where it hid. "Are you here for me to sign the papers?"

She stilled. Her breathing slowed. "Are you ready to sign?"

Her voice sounded uncertain. He prayed his ears weren't playing tricks. That he wasn't reading her wrong. The image of her walking away formed in his head sending a dagger into his heart. Good, bad, he had to know. Either way, the moment to be completely truthful had come.

"I'll never be. But if it's what you want, I will."

She leaned forward to rest her hand on his knee. Every nerve ending in his entire body tingled. "Oh, Samuel. It's not my choice. The decision has to be yours, not mine."

Sammy took her hand in his, scooted closer. "I understand. I just need to know if there's a chance. Any chance."

"I'll always want to be your friend. I'm going to—"

"Hey, Sammy." The tip of a crutch pushed the front door open. "I need your help again. My stupid car won't—" Kelsey hobbled in and froze. Her eyes shifted from one to the other. "Oops."

Kelsey swiveled to leave. The movement caused her crutch to slip on the hardwood floor. Her arms flailed as she lost her balance. She grabbed at the chair but slid to the floor.

Sammy slid his arms under hers. She leaned into him to push herself up and plopped her into the chair.

"Here." Tiff picked up the crutches.

"Thanks. I'm such a klutz. You must be Tiffany. Sorry to interrupt." She positioned the crutch. "I'll just go now."

"Wait," Sammy said. "I've been wanting you two to meet." Both women shot *are you crazy* looks at him.

He waved Tiff back to the couch. "This is Kelsey. The one I told you about."

Tiff studied her face again. "I think we met at the quilters meeting last year. Sorry I didn't recognize you."

Sammy was sure the remnants of Kelsey's black eye didn't help.

"Right. I never made the connection when Sammy told me about you either."

"It's a God thing. You two need to talk. Tiff needs crafters for a new project and you need a job."

Lame, but it moved them away from the topic of divorce.

"What kind of project?" Kelsey asked.

"I created a mixed media rendering of the Cliffs of Moher in Ireland. My business manager thinks it's something that would do well mass-produced. I need crafters to help produce comparable items of local and national icons."

"I've always done quilting."

"Learning to weave wouldn't be hard or the design could be adapted to quilting. Is it something you think you'd be interested in?"

"Absolutely."

Tension melted between Sammy's shoulders, and the muscles in his back unknotted. He shoved the divorce papers into a kitchen drawer. They'd talk about that another day.

"That's terrific! Do you have time to come out to the farm? I'll show you some examples?" She winked at him. "We'll finish our conversation one of these days."

"If Sammy can take me. My stupid car is on the blitz again. Mike is sending someone for it."

"I have a meeting, but I could pick you up if Aidan and Tiff took you."

"Sure." Tiff dug out her phone from her bag. "Let me call Aidan."

When Aidan arrived, Tiff wrapped her arms around Sammy's neck and pulled his head down for a kiss on the cheek. "Thank you. See you later."

The early evening air held a chill. Her lips were warm. His head spun from the rush he felt for her. Being around Tiff was like walking in quicksand.

Chapter 16

"Have you known Samuel long?" Tiffany asked Kelsey as they settled in the backseat. Aidan tucked her crutches into the trunk.

"No. I only moved in last week." Looking as if she were one blink away from waterworks, Kelsey shifted toward the window where fences of green fields lined with sunflowers replaced city buildings. "It's only temporary until I figure out what to do with my life. Sammy's been such a tremendous help."

Aidan's gaze met Tiffany's in the rearview mirror. She lifted her shoulder in a dismissive shrug. Aidan had been singing Samuel's praises ever since he met him. "He was always a great sounding board. Even as a little kid when we first met."

Kelsey shifted to face her. "He said you were married. What happened? He's such a great guy."

"He is. Was. Life interrupted. We've wandered apart. And I met someone else."

"I guess that happens but man, Sammy is everything I'd want in a husband. If I were married to him, I'd never let him go."

Though she had no claims on Samuel, a surge of possessiveness tightened Tiffany's chest and fired another dart at her troubling doubts about Brendan. She dismissed it with a slight shrug. Her gaze went to Kelsey's wedding ring. "Aren't you married already?"

Kelsey twisted the band on her finger, nodding. "But Jax is no Sammy. That's for sure."

Aidan turned off the main road and the farmhouse came into view. Kelsey sucked in a noisy breath. "Wow! This is where you work? It's lovely. I'd never get anything done. I'd sit in one of those rockers sipping coffee from sunrise to sunset. I bet the sky is gorgeous in the mornings and evenings."

"It is. That porch is one of the reasons I bought the place." Aidan opened her door as Tiffany's phone rang. "I need to take this. Can you help Kelsey while I talk? And put Moo on the screened porch. With her crutches, I'm not sure meeting Moo is a good idea."

She hadn't told Aidan she was investigating Brendan yet. They were nearly family. She didn't want to offend him, but when his research turned up two of their overseas supply factories were Mr. Choi's, she could no longer deny Brendan had lied about knowing the man. She needed to know what else he was hiding.

"Sure, and I will." He rounded the car with Kelsey's crutches. "Here you be."

Tiffany walked toward the large oak in the front yard. "Tiffany Fischer."

"I have that file ready if you want to come into the office," the voice said.

A shiver ran down her spine. She straightened. "I'm

in the middle of something now. Will tomorrow work?"

"Absolutely. You want to come here or tell me where and when and I'll meet you?"

She gave him the address for Backwoods. *It was done.* She'd tell Aidan tonight. He would understand. He'd cautioned her from the beginning to be careful with the man. She should have paid more attention. She hadn't. Now she'd have to fix things. Squaring her shoulders, she went inside.

Kelsey and Aidan stood at her quilting hoop. "Sorry about that."

Hearing her voice, Moo yipped.

"I feel bad you're locking up your dog. You should let her out. I love dogs. Jax didn't or I would have had one," Kelsey said.

"She's more like a small calf." Aidan chuckled. "Moo and those crutches wouldn't mix well."

"Exactly. That's why she's not coming in," Tiffany said.

"I'll be taking her for a walk. You ladies want tea or coffee before I go?"

Moo let out another wail. Tiffany shooed him with waving hands. "Go. I'll tend to us."

With a salute-turned-wave, Aidan left. Tiffany motioned Kelsey to the couch. "Tell me about your quilts."

She dug a photo album from the bag Samuel had grabbed for her before they left. Tiffany sat beside her as she described each quilt pictured. Kelsey had created with quilts what Tiffany did with her mixed media pieces. Each quilt told a family story same as her creation for Ms. Moore.

"These are amazing. It's the same idea I use to create family pieces for others." She took an album from her shelf. "See?"

"You know I never thought of using jewelry or gloves and lace collars. These are remarkable. What a treasure for the families."

"They are. And, I think it's a great idea for another new product line at Fischer. But not something to mass produce. Each piece would be unique from what the client provided."

"Yes. But it would take time. My quilts take months. These smaller pieces weeks."

"Well, we'll probably need to speed up or have more people to make any money." She studied Kelsey's face. "That is, if you wanted to make them to sell."

"You know, I was telling Sammy today, I needed to find something if I'm going to support myself. This wouldn't pay enough by itself. I'd have to find a real job, but it'd sure be something I'd love to do."

"Maybe you wouldn't need a second job."

From there the two brainstormed ideas for how to organize and run the project. She tuned out Brendan's voice in her head, "*Here you go again rescuing another mangy, flea-bitten underdog, throwing away money.*"

He'd never understood with the insurance settlement from the accident, she didn't have money worries. Kelsey did. Tiffany might not know the details of her story, but the heavy makeup on her cheeks and yellowish tone on her forearms shouted, "*help me.*" Her eyes, like a feral cat's, said the rest. Tiffany wanted to help and could help with or without Brendan's approval.

"Would you consider supervising this part of the business for me?"

"Are you serious?" Kelsey nodded. "It would be an answer to all my prayers. I might be able to leave Jax. I'm going to talk to Faith."

"Faith as in Samuel's sister?"

"Yes. She did a talk at the Post Chapel about legal rights and how to—" Her voice grew scratchy, and she made a business out of smoothing her skirt before continuing, "leave a marriage when you know you should."

Tiffany scooted closer and wrapped her arm around Kelsey's shoulders. "Call her right now. I'll help any way I can."

Kelsey pulled her phone from her purse.

Tiffany slipped into the kitchen to give her privacy. Minutes later, beaming, Kelsey joined her in the kitchen. "I did it. She's drawing up the papers."

"As Aidan would say in his Irish 'good on ya, girl.' I know it wasn't easy to give up on your marriage."

Doubts and questions about her relationship with Brendan had plagued her ever since Samuel returned. She struggled to know what to do. Hopefully, tomorrow's meeting would give her some clear direction.

"I called Sammy to come to get me. He should be here soon."

"Want to sit on the front porch while we wait?"

"I'd really like to meet Moo before I go. I feel bad that I'm the reason she's locked out."

"Tell you what, after we get you settled in one of the rocking chairs, I'll bring her around."

"It's a deal." Grinning, Kelsey tucked the crutches under her arms and headed for the front door.

Tiffany followed a few minutes later with Moo on a lead. "Sit." The Panda-bear-looking dog sat in front of Kelsey and raised her paw.

"Hello, Moo. Jax never would let me have a dog. Now I can get one. Maybe not one as big as you, though."

"But this one is a gentle giant. Aren't you, girl?"

The voice from behind her had Tiffany stiffening. She turned slowly and pasted a smile on her face. Her pulse jumped. He smelled of soap, plain generic soap without a scent. His hair, dark and thick, peeked around his ear lobe. Her fingers itched to brush the curls from his ear, off his forehead. Samuel Fitzpatrick would always make her heart thump, her blood race every time she saw him. She took a moment to let the air go in and out of her lungs. "Samuel."

Their gazes clung. Unsettling silence, loaded with memories and feelings, danced around them.

"How'd it go?" he asked, breaking the spell.

"Tiffany offered me a job." Kelsey's voice bubbled. "And..." she leaned over to ruffle Moo's chin. "I've decided to get a dog."

He shot Tiffany a questioning look.

"I'm not sure about the dog. I did offer the job. We're going to launch a line that combines my mix-media memory projects with her quilt-memory pieces. She's a perfect match to run the new line."

Kelsey balanced on one leg to hug her. "I promise I won't let you down."

Tiffany put Moo on a sit-stay command and carried

Kelsey's tote to the car. "We'll firm things up after I talk to my business manager." She passed the tote to her when she settled in the front seat.

Sammy slammed the car door. "Thank you for helping her out. She desperately needed a break. Together we would have been an awesome team in Guatemala." He winked and rounded the car.

Remorse settled on her shoulders as she watched his taillights disappear. Things might have been so different she'd chosen to contact him after the accident.

Chapter 17

A reef of clouds and lightning raced across the skies on the way to Backwoods the next day. A clap of thunder roared close by, and rain sheeted the windshield conjuring up unwanted memories. Tiffany's hands shook, and her body shivered.

"Relax. It's supposed to clear up by noon," Aidan offered reassurances like he always did when they had to go out on rainy days. Mostly, they canceled plans and stayed in if the weather was like this. Today she couldn't, she had to get this over with and make her decision. Judge Hunt's deadline was fast approaching.

Aidan stopped at the entrance of Backwoods and helped her inside. "Hang tight. I'll get the umbrella then move the car and be right back."

She tucked her bag under her arm and gripped the straps to still her hand. The air was dense and cool. Pine trees shook in the wind and scattered pine needles across the entrance. A solitary drop of water struck her head, hard, like a marble—an omen?

She ducked under the covered doorway to wait for Aidan. After she'd told him what she'd done on the drive, he'd wanted him to hear what the investigator had found too and reminded her of his caution about becoming so involved with Brendan. Aidan came running, shook the umbrella, propped it against the wall. "Let's hope we're both wrong," he said then opened the front door.

Tiffany spotted a man seated in the corner looking toward the entrance and led the way. She'd never met Jim Gunn but he fit her stereo-typical image of a private investigator, tight sport jacket, his back to the wall, and his eyes watching the entrance.

He stood as they approached and extended his hand. "Jim Gunn."

"Tiffany Fischer and this is Aidan Callahan."

The server brought coffee and took their orders after she and Aidan sat across from Mr. Gunn. They chatted casually about the weather and current events while they ate. As soon as the server cleared the dishes and refilled the coffee mugs, Mr. Gunn pulled a folder from his leather satchel on the chair beside him and laid it on the table. "Mr. Murphy's file. You didn't explain why you wanted me to check the man out, but after looking into his business dealings, I'd be wary."

"And didn't I say the same thing even though I'd hoped he'd changed." Aidan rolled his eyes.

"What do you mean?"

"Some of his business contacts are on the FBI watch list for human trafficking."

She gasped.

"There's no proof. But where there's smoke, there's usually fire to coin a phrase."

"Do you think he'd be a part of it?" Aidan asked. "He

used to run with those types but never participated."

"I can't say positively yes or no. I don't see evidence he's actively participating."

"I can't believe he'd be involved," Tiffany said.

"Again, it could be he's clever and knows how to operate behind the scenes. Or he's being coerced. They have something on him. That happens a lot."

Aidan nodded his head. "Now that, I could believe. Brendan pushes limits. Back home he was always in trouble with the Garda. That's why he came over for a fresh start."

"Being involved with these men is not a fresh start. He's asking for trouble."

Tiffany set her mug on the table. "Are any of the suspected vendors connected to Fischer Textiles?"

Mr. Gunn lifted the file and thumbed through the pages. "This one, for sure. He's a convicted human trafficker. Unfortunately, he got off with a light sentence which is why he's out building his cover businesses again." Gunn placed the sheet between her and Aidan.

Tiffany recognized the letterhead of Mr. Choi's factory in Guatemala. She rubbed her thumb over her clenched fist. After she'd specifically told Brendan to wait, he'd signed an agreement with Choi.

Aidan placed a hand over hers. "We can cancel that contract, right? Fischer Textile doesn't want to be associated with him if he's suspected again."

"Your agreement is dated one day ago. You'd have to check with a lawyer, but you should have forty-eight hours to reconsider."

Anger blurred her vision. She struggled to find her

voice. Closing the file, she gathered it in her hands and tapped it on the tabletop "Thank you, Mr. Gunn."

"If you need anything else, give me a call." He pushed back, took his satchel, and left.

"I'm so sorry. I'd hoped Brendan had changed. I should not have let you turn the business over to him."

Tiffany gripped his arm as he stood. "No. I should have listened to your warning, and Brendan should have listened to me when I told him not to do business with Mr. Choi. He lied to me. Time to set him straight."

"I'll get the car."

She jerked her engagement ring off her finger and dropped it in the zipper pocket in her purse then signed off on the receipt the server brought her and followed Aidan to the exit.

"Take me to Brendan's," she said as she settled in the car.

Muttering "I don't think this is a good idea," Aidan drove her to Brendan's downtown office as she asked. He pulled to the curb and Tiffany hopped out before he could get around the car.

"Tiffany, wait. You need to calm down."

She ignored him. The raindrops spotted her blouse as she dashed to the building. She headed straight to the elevators. Brendan stood blocking her exit when the doors slid open on the third floor.

"Your office." She sidestepped him and headed straight past the open-mouthed secretary and stopped cross-armed in the center of his glass-walled office.

Brendan trailed behind, closing the door. "Tiffany,

Luv." He said her name with the heavy Irish cadence that had charmed her at their introduction. Well, now she knew him to be more like an Irish traveler. Lying and cheating to make a buck.

She glared at him. "You signed that agreement with Choi even though I asked you not to."

"Well, you see, I'd be—"

"No, I don't see. I will not collaborate with a man who runs a sweatshop. Certainly never one who's served time for human trafficking."

Branden's posture seemed to melt. His shoulders drooped then popped back up. "No. You're wrong. There's been a mistake."

"I'm right. I hired a private investigator. You've been lying to me."

"You did what? How dare you!"

"How dare I? It's my company. We had a partnership agreement. But you've misled me, and I'm hiring a lawyer to end that."

"But...I promise I did not know Mr. Choi...I..."

"Another lie. Samuel told you what his shops were like. That should have been enough to make you avoid any business deals with him. Instead, you signed that new agreement behind my back. I'm through, Brendan. With the partnership and us." She fished the ring from her purse, threw it at him, and met Aidan coming off the elevator.

Her arm slid through his twirling him around. "I'm ready to leave."

Chapter 18

A week went by and Sammy didn't hear from Tiff. He kept himself busy helping Chaplain Mike. But all the while she'd been on his mind. It was a deep ache that started in his heart and leaked out to every nerve in his body.

He'd thought about calling her but stopped himself. She needed to be the one to reach out. Faith reminded him, he'd stated his case and told her he would always love her. The ball was in Tiff's court.

But a call hadn't come. His love didn't matter.

Kelsey wasn't around as much either. She'd met with Faith. With the separation official, she'd found a place of her own. Then she'd gotten a rescue pup, an adorable little mutt, a mix between a poodle and wire-haired terrier with pointy whiskers sticking out all over his snout. She'd turned her life around.

It was time he did too.

He pulled his car into the parking space in front of Blake and Faith's quarters at Ft. Bragg and rested his forehead on the steering wheel. Time for him to cut the ties of the past and... do what else, he didn't know. He picked up the large manila envelope and went to the door.

Faith answered. "Come in."

He handed her the envelope. "Not this morning. I need to get on down the road. I've got a long drive ahead of me."

Coming to North Carolina had been a breeze because he'd expected to be making this return drive with Tiffany. Going back home without her would be next to unbearable. He'd need to pull himself together before he faced his family.

"You could stay here until after the hearing. Say your goodbyes."

"It's better this way."

He'd gone to the farm to give her the papers in person. Brendan had been there. Tiffany in his arms, kissing her. The sight of them together had been too much. Sammy had backed out of the driveway before they saw him and came straight here.

Faith hugged him. "Be patient, little brother. God has a soulmate for you."

"I know." He would always believe it was Tiffany, even if God hadn't answered his prayers and she chose Brendan. "See you at the big reception Mom's planning in a few weeks."

Ava came around the corner. "You're not leaving without telling me goodbye, are you?"

"Never."

"Sorry. It didn't work out like you'd wanted. You'll find the right one."

"You could leave Thad." He winked.

Ava laughed and her body shook. "Not gonna happen. He's a keeper. If he weren't, I'd take you up on it." She handed him a Tupperware container of cookies. "These'll help make the drive easier. Be safe."

"I hope you saved some for us," Faith whined.

"Of course. You got the coffee ready?"

With a final hug to both, Sammy climbed into his car.

Tiffany scanned the courtroom from her seat on the thick upholstered bench in the public seating area. Blake and Faith sat on the other side. Samuel must have stepped out or hadn't arrived yet.

Aidan gripped her hand and whispered, "It's going to be fine."

She wasn't convinced. She wished she'd been available to talk with Samuel. With long meetings every day separating her company from Brendan's, there just hadn't been any time. Besides what she needed to say shouldn't be said over the phone.

"All rise." The bailiff's voice bellowed into the deafening silence.

Judge Hunt in his bat-like robes swept in and sat, looking as fearsome as ever. The first case was called. Her new lawyer, Mr. Spafford, motioned for her to remain seated.

Two other lawyers went through the squeaky gate to approach the bench as the bailiff called two more numbers. After short discussions, they left with their clients.

The clerk called Fischer vs Fitzpatrick case number.

Her new lawyer popped up. Tiffany leaned forward to look over where Blake and Faith sat. Still no Samuel.

Aidan squeezed her hand as she rose. Spafford waved her to the plaintiff's table before he approached Judge Hunt. After a brief discussion, the judge motioned Blake to the bench.

Tiffany glanced over at Faith who returned an *I-don't-know* shrug.

Judge Hunt leaned forward as the conversation continued. Finally, he raised his gavel. "Case dismissed."

The gavel came down with a bang that rang in Tiffany's ears. Judge Hunt winked at her. "And best wishes to the couple."

The two lawyers walked away shaking hands. Tiffany glanced at Faith. Her expression looked as baffled as Tiffany felt.

"Follow me," her lawyer said. Blake motioned Faith to come along. Aidan's mouth gaped as he joined the parade from the courtroom.

"What just happened?" Faith glared at Blake.

"Where's Samuel?" Tiffany asked.

Blake waved them toward the exit. "Let's take this outside. We can talk there."

Faith whorled on Blake as soon as they reached the benches around a fountain in front of the building. "What did he mean he wished the couple well? Sammy signed the divorce papers."

Tiffany's chest squeezed until she couldn't breathe. *Samuel signed the divorce papers.* She sank to the bench. She'd taken too long.

"What'd ya mean he signed? He loves the lass. Clear

as the nose on ya face." Aidan's voice twined with disbelief and anger.

"Exactly." Blake nodded. "That's why when Mr. Spafford said Tiffany hadn't signed, I decided to ignore Sammy's wishes. Now we need to figure out how to tell him." His gaze locked with Tiffany's. "Unless you want to tell him yourself."

"But if he signed, he must want a divorce." She sagged against the back of the bench.

"No, no, no. He's never wanted a divorce. He said he told you that," Faith argued.

"He must have changed his mind. Otherwise, why did he sign?"

Faith rolled her eyes heavenward. "Because he thought that was what you wanted. He did not look happy when he came by to drop off the papers and say goodbye."

"He's gone back to Texas?" Tiffany's heart cracked. "It's too late."

Aidan sat beside her on the bench and patted her leg. "Never too late. We'll follow him to Texas."

"Wait." Faith grinned. "That's not necessary. I have a better idea. You should surprise him at our wedding reception."

"Your wedding reception? Didn't you already have that?"

"One, here at the Officer's Club for Blake's friends, but most of my siblings—remember there are eight of us, couldn't all come. Mom planned a party aka reception at the church for our friends and family. You and Aidan should join us."

Quiet hovered as Tiffany thought about Faith's idea.

"I'm thinking it'd be a lovely surprise," Aidan encouraged her.

She smiled. "It'll be perfect."

Chapter 19

Two weeks later, Tiffany waited off to the side as the New Hope Community Church Fellowship Hall filled with familiar faces and lots of new ones. Here in this very room, she and Samuel had played chase, shared kisses in the kitchen during Caleb and Carrie's wedding and plotted their elopement during a prayer meeting. Lots of their memories centered here. She prayed today would be another.

A good one.

But her life and her work were in North Carolina. Samuel's life was in Guatemala or wherever the mission board sent him plus all his family lived here. How would that work? Would he leave all this for her? Could she move her business to Texas?

She spotted Samuel talking to Josh and Mara, his back to her. The three of them surrounded by a group of young boys from the home. Samuel's unruly hair gave him away. Butterflies danced with dragonflies in her stomach. What if Faith was wrong and Samuel had genuinely wanted his freedom and leaving the signed papers was his way of saying goodbye?

Josh tipped his head toward her and Samuel turned. Second thoughts bunched in her throat until a smile spread across Samuel's face. "He's coming this way."

Aidan grinned like a proud Irish shadchan. "I told you he's been looking for ya."

"You weren't supposed to say anything."

"Who's saying I did? I can be saying the same for Faith."

 "What if—"

"Stop. I'm sure he only signed the papers because you were engaged to Brendan. Now you're not and Brendan's gone. Take my advice. Give him a chance to explain before ya keep making assumptions."

Samuel slowly made his way toward them. Aidan slipped away when he reached her. As Samuel's sparkling blue eyes met hers, his smile grew until it filled her entire field of vision. She blinked. The smile was still there and her heart beat triple time.

"I can't believe you're here," he said. "I thought I'd never see you again."

Her breath caught at the simple, direct statement. "I wanted to see you. These weeks have been the worst weeks of my life."

He took her hand. "Let's go out in the courtyard."

An early cold front had dipped the temperature in the short time since she'd arrived. She shivered in the chilly air. Samuel quickly slipped off his jacket to wrap it around her shoulders.

His heat still clung to his coat. It was as though his arms were around her. "Why'd you sign the divorce papers?" Best to tackle the elephant and get on with it.

"I thought it was what you wanted." He gazed into her eyes. "Wasn't it?"

"No. But I couldn't tell you until I got things sorted with Brendan."

His gaze drifted to her left hand.

"It's gone. I'd been questioning a marriage to Brendan long before you arrived. After you brought up Mr. Choi, I realized more than a marriage troubled me." She paused to pull his jacket tighter around her. "I hired a private investigator and learned he'd signed the agreement with Choi behind my back. And sadly, it wasn't the first sweatshop Brendan used. It's taken time to fix all that, but he's gone for good from my life and Fischer Textiles."

His arm circled her shoulder tucking her head into the crook of his neck. "I can't say I'm sorry. Not since it's brought you home."

She felt warm and safe with his breath in her hair. "I love you, Samuel. I have since you proposed on this very bench all those years ago."

"I never stopped loving you." He straightened and slid to his knee in front of her. "I don't have a ring this time, but will you marry me?"

She lifted the chain around her neck and pulled out her wedding ring from inside her dress. "I brought it just in case."

She undid the clasp and dropped the ring into his hand. "If only I'd contacted you after the accident, we wouldn't have lost all those years."

His finger gently tapped her lips. "The past is over."

He slipped the ring on her finger. Pulling her into his

arms, he kissed her forehead softly. "And now we have the rest of our lives."

Samuel cupped her cheeks and slid his hands along her jaw. His eyes never left hers as he tilted her face toward him. His lips met hers in a kiss filled with all the love that was meant to be. A love that had lasted ten years and would carry them into forever.

Applause and cheers exploded behind them. The wolf whistles penetrated Samuel's brain. They pivoted to see the Fitzpatrick clan along with Aidan watching.

Pastor Fitz's voice rose above the noise. He circled to stand behind them. "It is my honor and privilege to do something I didn't get to do the first time." Cupping his hands on their shoulders, he grinned. "I present to you, Mr. and Mrs. Sammy Fitzpatrick."

Blake was the first to come forward with congratulations. "And, you know the best part? We don't have to go through all those wedding preparations again. You're already married."

Faith nodded. "Amen."

Ms. Pat frowned. "Well, I for one will miss all that. I love a good wedding and reception."

"You love any party, dear." Pastor Fitz chuckled. "Think of all the anniversaries and birthday parties you'll get to plan and the grandbabies that will join little Benjamin."

"True. Let's go share the good news with our guests." Hand-in-hand the older couple disappeared inside. The other siblings and their spouses took turns offering good wishes then joined their parents.

Sammy stopped Blake and Faith. "Thank you both."

"Just returning the favor," Faith said. "Is it too soon to ask if you're going to move to North Carolina or Tiffany's coming here?"

Blake's arm went around her waist and twirled her toward the church. "Yes. Time for us to mingle with our guests and let these two make plans."

Sammy sat and pulled Tiff down beside him on the bench. "It is a good question. I think I should move to Fayetteville."

"*Really*? What about your work at Greenvine? I watched you interacting with the boys. You love them and they love you."

"I do, and I'll miss them, especially Tucker, but they have great support systems with Mara and Josh and Burt and Rose, the caregivers at Greenvine.."

"Mara told me Faith's working on adoption papers for her and Josh. Tucker's gonna be fine. A big brother and a dog named Bear. It's all a boy could want."

"True. And we could bring all of them to Fayetteville for summer vacation or one of the school breaks."

"Moo would like that."

Sammy squirmed a bit. "I'd still need a job. I was thinking you might need more help with the business now that you-know-who's gone."

"But you would have to give up your mission work."

"I already did when I started helping Mara at Greenvine. Lots of broken families and many women, and men, out there like Kelsey. It's my new mission. I was thinking Fischer Textile could do more to help others like her."

"I've been trying to do that all along. Brendan kinda

sidetracked me. Let's do it. One more thing…" she pressed her lips together. "Are you good with accounting? I do hate the business part."

"Yeah. Kinda. I can learn." He grinned.

"It's settled then. North Carolina, here we come."

Chapter 20

One year later...

"I'm sure." Restraining the urge to scream, Tiffany huffed the words at Aidan and her husband. "I promised Faith I'd be there and I will be. Fort Bragg's not that far to drive."

"But it's a lot further than those little jaunts we've been doing," Sammy argued.

"He's right," Aidan said. "There'll be traffic."

"I can do it." Okay, maybe she wasn't exactly positive she could, but she knew for sure either of them would come rescue her if she had to stop.

Once she and Sammy returned, he and Aidan encouraged her to drive more, taking on her regular practice drives.

Yes, she'd started calling her husband Sammy not Samuel like everyone else. Samuel was far too formal for the easy-going man she lived with. And loved with all her heart.

They'd started with short drives down the long driveway to the road and progressed to trips to Backwoods and grocery shopping. It hadn't been easy at first and she didn't think she'd ever be able to drive in a rainstorm. She could barely ride in the backseat during one.

But the sun was shining today and she had promised Faith and Kelsey she'd talk to the group about job opportunities with Fischer Textiles.

"Take care of them while I'm gone." She patted Moo and then looked up at the two men. "No following me just to be sure I make it. Understood? I'll text when I get there." They nodded.

Her hand shook a bit as she clicked the start button on the car key fob. She squeezed the door handle to steady her nerves. There was no physical reason she couldn't drive. She'd known that for years.

She could do this.

As she headed down her driveway, she checked the side mirror. Sammy and Aidan stood on the front porch like twins, with hands in their pockets watching, concern written all over their faces, and wrinkles lining their foreheads. She tapped on the horn twice and turned onto the highway.

That night lying in bed beside Sammy she rolled over and kissed him. "Thank you."

He turned on his side and propped his cheek on his hand. "What for?"

"For helping me to drive again. For waiting when I never contacted you. For running Fischer Textiles."

He leaned down and kissed her forehead. "When I promised in front of that Justice of the Peace that I'd love you forever, I meant it. I hated signing those papers. Hardest thing I've ever done."

"Why did you?"

"That day I went out to the farm to ask you one more time to reconsider and break off your engagement. I turned onto your driveway and saw you and Brendan kissing on the porch, I decided God was giving me a sign and did a U-turn. I took the papers to Faith and Blake to take to court and headed back home. I'm so very thankful Blake had the wisdom to lie to Judge Hunt and tell him I hadn't signed either."

She ran a finger along his cheek. "Oh, Sammy. If you'd waited for half a second longer that day, you'd have seen me slap the tarnation out of Brendan."

"Huh?"

"My lawyer had delivered the papers dissolving our business partnership, and Brendan had come to force some sense into me. That's what the kiss was all about. He was lucky Aidan and Moo were out in the pasture or Moo would have bitten him and Aidan would have punched his lights out."

"Aidan told me he tried to warn you about getting involved with him."

"He did. I wouldn't listen. Brendan was such a successful entrepreneur. And a real charmer. I trusted him. I didn't pay attention like I should have —signed stuff I didn't read—or it never would have happened." She kissed him again. "I'm thrilled you manage all that stuff for me."

He stuck his lip out in a pout. "Is that the only reason you keep me?"

"Of course not, silly." She reached over him and turned off the bedside lamp

Author's Note

Dear Reader,

Thank you so much for reading When Love Comes Home. If you'd like to make sure you never miss a new release, sign up for my newsletter at https://judythemorgan. com/ and please like my Facebook page at https://www. facebook.com/JudytheMorgan/

Most importantly, recommend the book to friends, readers' groups, and discussion boards so other readers can find it. Word of mouth is incredibly important for helping other readers discover new authors.

If you enjoyed Sammy and Tiffany's story, please help others find and enjoy the book, too. Write a review and post on GoodReads or Amazon to tell other readers why you liked this book.

I appreciate all reviews whether positive, negative or somewhere in-between.

Until next time!

Judythe

Acknowledgments

Thanks to Kim Ford, Stacey Purcell, and Stephanie Wayman the best critique/writing partners ever.

And special hugs and thanks to my husband, who is the role model for all my heroes, my most trusted story editor, and eagle-eyed copy editor.
Love you, always and forever.

About the Author

Judythe Morgan is a native Texan whose roots called her home after years of roaming as an Air Force daughter and then Army wife. Now, she writes award-winning stories of second chances, forgiveness, and happy endings full-time.

You'll find plenty of twists and turns for her characters drawn from her experiences as a schoolteacher, an antique dealer, a former mayor's wife, and sometimes church pianist.

Enjoy her stories written from a Christian worldview and filled with strong characters tackling real-life situations. Besides fiction, she blogs weekly at www.judythewriter.com

Sign up for her free newsletter at https://judythemorgan.com/ to keep up with her latest news and subscriber-only sneak peeks. Friend her on Facebook and Goodreads and follow her on Twitter.

OTHER TITLES IN THIS INSPIRATIONAL SERIES:

Book 1, When Love Blooms – Andy & Darcy
Book 2, Love Returns – Becca & Ethan
Book 3, When Love Endures – Sarah & Nick
Book 4, When Love Trusts – Josh & Mara
Book 5, When Love Wins – Faith & Blake

Also by Judythe

Seeing Clearly
Thrilling suspense and seasoned romance

Ex-cop Dawson McKey is consumed by revenge after a cartel's bomb kills his twin sons. He trusts no one and vows payback. He refuses to get close to anyone, let alone fall in love again. But widow Evie Parker challenges his thinking. She's raising her grandson after her only child and his wife die in a suspicious car accident and it's taking a toll.

Alarms go off in Dawson's head when Evie receives threatening emails concerning her grandson. Then Evie's nanny disappears with her grandson. Dawson knows something is deadly wrong.

Pushed to their limits searching for the toddler, will Dawson and Evie learn seeing clearly is the only way to live and love?

Claiming Annie's Heart
An Irish Love Story

Annie Foster stays in Ireland after boarding school to nanny a widower's infant daughter. Five years later, the widower proposes.

Her first love Chad Jones, whom she believes abandoned her, arrives weeks before the wedding on an undercover assignment probing her fiancé's connection with IRA terrorists. Chad's determined to change Annie's mind and her heart because he's never stopped loving her.

Which man will claim Annie's heart?

The Promise Series

Two men and one woman met at Eighth Army Headquarters, South Korea in the turbulent Vietnam War years and their lives are irreversibly linked. The promises they made to themselves and each other bind their hearts forever.

Book 1, Love in the Morning Calm
Book 2, The Pendant's Promise
Book 3, Until He Returns
Book 4, Promises to Keep